Swan Songs

Swan Songs

B. Elizabeth Beck

Accents Publishing • Lexington, Kentucky • 2025

Printed in the United States of America

Accents Publishing
Editor: Katerina Stoykova
Cover Painting: Group IX/SUW, *The Swan*, No. 1 (1915) by Hilma af Klint

Library of Congress Control Number: 2025940121
ISBN: 978-1-961127-16-6
First Edition

Accents Publishing is an independent press for brilliant voices. For a catalog of current and upcoming titles, please visit us on the Web at

www.accents-publishing.com

CONTENTS

All I know is something like a bird within her sang

—Robert Hunter

See Here How Everything

"Don't *Grandma* me. You know damn well I won't answer to anything other than Bertha," the old woman snarls at her granddaughter.

The younger woman nods as she opens the curtains. Miranda studies the early morning sunshine slanting on the pine floorboards her grandfather installed when they built this house in Laurel Canyon. He is long gone, but his memory exists in every corner of the custom house he lovingly constructed for his bride, who dreamed of a romance like Joni Mitchell and Graham Nash. Maybe it was Stephen Stills. Miranda can never remember much of what her grandmother says. Her grandmother, whose actual name is Ethel and not Bertha, for the record, reminisces about her Grateful Dead days while Miranda purposefully tunes her out. If this new applicant for a home health aide doesn't pass muster, Miranda doesn't know what she will do. This is the seventh interview in as many days, and no matter how many times Miranda emphasizes to the agency how important the aide's taste in music affects their chances at employment, not one candidate can answer the golden question: who is Jerry Garcia?

There is no way the university will extend Miranda's sabbatical past next semester, especially considering her lack of publications to show her time was productive. It was productive, but not from an academic sense. Bertha would say it was cosmic timing that she had a series of strokes the day after Miranda closed her office door and left campus, intending to finally complete her research. Of course, Miranda's mother, Cassidy, can't be counted on to help.

Miranda sighs before turning to Bertha to begin the laborious task of bathing and dressing the old woman. She swallows her resentment that Cassidy's endeavor to travel with a band called Phish to sell tie-dyes is more significant than Miranda's tenure-track position as a professor of English. What other family thinks like that? The hippie on tour with a band, doing God only knows what drugs is in higher esteem than the black sheep who had the nerve to pursue an MFA in creative writing, publish three collections of poetry with small but prestigious presses, and have the further audacity to sign a contract to teach for a formal academic institution to pay the bills. No matter how many times Miranda cites Allen Ginsberg, Lawrence Ferlinghetti and mentions City Lights Bookstore, Bertha rolls her eyes and says, "They had nothing on Robert Hunter. You know, he was a direct descendent of Robert Burns. What? Burns isn't good enough for you, Miz Brainiac?"

As she helps Bertha to the bathroom, Miranda studies the framed photograph of Jerry Garcia she mistook as a picture of her grandfather until she was five years old and could decipher the letters of the autograph that did not spell Jacob Pratt, her grandfather's name. Although she only has vague memories of the man since he died when she was three, it was Miranda's first tug of resentment. The frustration at her misunderstanding still burns as a tiny flame in the recesses of Miranda's thirty-year-old brain. The back of her memories, the lyric instinctually leaps to her consciousness, much like another Grateful Dead song triggers while reading *scarlet begonia* printed on a white plastic label in a garden center. Miranda mentally responds, *daydream* every time she hears *sunshine*. She can't help it. It's infused in her genes.

Using organic chamomile soap infused with lavender Bertha receives on trade from a woman named Rainbow, Miranda carefully washes her grandmother's body with a hemp sponge before lathering her in patchouli oil and dressing Bertha in one of the several caftans she now favors. Combing Bertha's long hair and winding it into a bun takes less time than patience. Miranda leaves Bertha to consider which jewelry she will choose from her vast collection; jewelry is crucial in her grandmother's life. Beading jewelry was her vocation and avocation, more her reason than her means for touring with the band. Being a vendor on Shakedown Street gives you a place of belonging. The holes Miranda's mother pierced in Miranda's ears when she was only a baby stand naked in protest. No vivid colors in her wardrobe; her teacher outfits consist of pencil skirts or tailored pants with simple knits, and cotton or silk shirts paired with leather loafers. Not one tie-dye in her closet and merely one strand of pearls Miranda clasps around her neck to teach. When she's not teaching, Miranda dons blue jeans and simple shirts or yoga pants because when she is not writing or teaching, she likes to practice yoga.

She stretches her neck, pulling her ear to her shoulder as the tea kettle on the stove boils, knowing the past three months of merely practicing yoga sporadically and not attending her regular classes are taking a toll on her muscles. Hell, it is wreaking havoc on her mind, too. There is only so much pot a person can smoke. When Miranda points out to Bertha that even Ram Dass stopped using psychedelics and started practicing meditation because he didn't like to come down, Bertha replies, "That's only because he didn't wait long enough for the bud these kids are growing and selling today. Long gone are the days of schwag, stems, and seeds. Come down? What's that?"

It's not as if Miranda doesn't like the Grateful Dead's music. It's not really about the music or the scene. Anything that takes her mother's attention away from Miranda is a source of anguish, a lingering pull children feel when abandoned. Of course, her mother wouldn't consider Miranda abandoned. Cassidy carried her daughter on her back as an infant, wandering from city to city to follow the band. It was a family affair for a while, including her grandfather and Bertha. But whenever Cassidy fell for a new man, Miranda was cast aside to her grandparent's care without a backward glance. Sometimes Cassidy would only be gone for days. Other times, weeks, and a few times, months. Because Miranda was told her mother was gone, on tour with the Grateful Dead, carefully omitting the part about Cassidy in yet another romance, Miranda resented the band. And it is embarrassing that Bertha inserts her ideas and hippie philosophies everywhere she goes, in every conversation she has. When three children rang the door to ask for a donation to travel to Costa Rica on a missionary trip, offering in return a wooden ornament printed with scripture. Bertha retrieved a ten-dollar bill from her pocket.

"I am not Christian, but I do believe in your faith to do what you think is good for the world and what I believe in most is kindness. So, take this money but keep your ornament. Go do good in the world, children. Fare thee well," Bertha said as she closed the door, and Miranda responded in rote, *my honey.*

The doorbell rings after breakfast in the garden where Bertha prefers to spend her days reading and listening to music, stretched on a lounge chair where she nods off to birds chirping; blue sky the last image before fatigue overtakes her senses while Miranda sits at the scrolled metal garden table, laptop open, empty document waiting to be imprinted with new verse she has yet to muster. Answering the door for this new candidate is a welcome interruption, even though Miranda dreads the inevitable. Bertha will cast sideways glances, dismiss the poor soul as unworthy, and pretend to fall asleep to end the interview early as Miranda politely makes excuses for her grandmother even though it isn't the strokes that changed her personality. Bertha has always been this way. The irony of the deadhead culture irks Miranda. Open-minded, liberal, enlightened people are as elitist from their perspective as the capitalistic, middle-class conservatives they criticize are. Status depends upon how many shows you have seen, what vehicle you drive (VW buses, Jeeps, and Subarus, the gold standard), whose tie-dye you wear (better be Cassidy Creations, or you're a poseur), and which strand of marijuana you smoke. There are more categories defining the "custies," short for customers, from the real heads, primarily vendors.

Consequently, dismissed were the young woman in a starched blouse with a Peter Pan collar, the older man in an actual suit and tie, and the middle-aged woman Miranda believed to be the most qualified candidate, unsuitable because she donned Gucci loafers and a Cartier watch. Bertha may never wear anything designer like that, but she could identify status immediately. "Must be a recent widow looking for something to do. Better off joining a million charities and devoting herself to endless fundraising than wanting to care for an old hippie like me," Bertha sniffed. After reading the woman's resume, Miranda saved that applicant's contact information. If whoever walked through this door didn't meet with Bertha's approval, Miranda has no choice. Bertha will just have to suffer the indignities of being washed by a woman wearing Brooks Brothers. Serves her right.

Determined to hire this new candidate, Miranda arranges for a preliminary meeting she plans to whisper in the front room before escorting the person through the back of the house, out to the garden where Bertha waits. Instead of an afternoon appointment like all the others, Miranda lies to Bertha and says this candidate can only meet in the morning, knowing Miranda could carve this private conversation easily while Bertha reclines in the garden. Practically the only thing Miranda can count on is Bertha's daily schedule. Its regularity mundane yet necessary to keep Bertha soothed. Any changes in routine or environment prompt Bertha to become so agitated that it takes Miranda hours and too many weed gummies, in Miranda's opinion, to quiet the old woman. Ironic for a nomadic woman. If Bertha went too many weeks without a live show, she would be so antsy that it drove her husband crazy, inevitably packing up the VW Bus, loading his wife and family, the tie-dyes, beads, jewelry, and supplies, and taking them on tour. Miranda wonders what he would think if he could see his wife now and returns to the recurring thought she hopes to shape into a poem. The heart attack that took Grandfather down was a perfect death, a clean death, if you will, especially compared to the devastation a series of small strokes have on a person, reduced to an infant almost in its diminished quality of life. Certainly in need of full-time care.

Miranda reaches for the door handle as the bell rings a second time. Standing on the front porch is what appears to be a perfect candidate. Blond hair cut not too short, bearded, with smiling eyes, wearing blue jeans and a plain hooded sweatshirt. Miranda spies a woven bracelet around his left wrist next to a watch and notices a glass pendant hanging from a hemp rope around the man's neck.

Miranda smiles at the young man and says, "Hello, you must be Jonathan. Please, come in."

Miranda settles in an armchair and indicates for Jonathan to take a seat on the sofa. Like most people upon their first visit, Jonathan hesitates, too busy gaping. Grandfather spared no expense in money and time to build his dream house. The sweeping front room with beveled glass windows reaching the top of the cathedral ceilings is impressive enough without the stained-glass transom windows above the doorways leading to other rooms of the house. Another wall features a stone fireplace flanked by bookshelves so high that a sliding ladder was installed. Stuffed between the vast collection of books and on the wood slab mantle are objects of art, vases, and sculptures her grandparents collected from friends and through their travels. Paintings and photographs, some framed and others not, dominate the only wall without doors or windows, hung so closely that the paint behind is barely visible. Miranda smiles when Jonathan spots the intricately beaded cobweb in the far-left corner of the room and walks toward it for further inspection. Not many people focus on one of the most exquisite pieces in the room, its web strung with crystal beads and pearls with tiny chandelier crystals mimicking dewdrops.

"How long have you worked as an aide with the agency?" Miranda asks, distracting Jonathan from the web and back to the matter at hand, his reason for being, this interview. Jonathan takes a seat on the sofa and replies, "Three years. My patient just passed away last month, so I'm looking for a new assignment."

When Miranda says, "Don't say *passed away*. Say *dead*," Jonathan looks startled. She also does not offer expected condolences. Good.

Better she surprises him first in preparation for the earthquake that is Bertha. Miranda needs this final applicant to be a good fit. There is barely time to wait. She shakes her head to dismiss the lyric and asks, "Who is Jerry Garcia?"

"Only the *Greatest Story Ever Told*," Jonathan replies correctly.

Miranda feels the crick in her neck disappear in relief. Not trusting in hope, she squints and asks, "What do you really know about the Grateful Dead?"

"I wasn't old enough to see Jerry on stage, regrettably. But I have seen Dead and Company thirty-two times. And I like JRAD and catch Phil and Friends whenever I can. Does that count?"

In response, Miranda stands and motions for Jonathan to follow her to the garden to meet Bertha, who would surely be ringing the bell at any moment to request tea or fruit, another book or an extra blanket, assistance to use the bathroom, or any of the multitude of tasks Miranda looks forward to entrusting to Jonathan if the interview continues as well as it started. They walk swiftly through the unused formal dining room into the kitchen, where Miranda pauses to point out the obvious. If he is hired, they will return to this room for detailed diet and medication instructions before Miranda takes him to the bedroom and bathroom, newly outfitted with rails, a seat in the shower, and everything else a stroke survivor needs to be safe.

Miranda squints in the sunlight as she pushes the screen door, Jonathan following. Bertha's lounge chair faces the garden, and as Miranda walks across the stone patio, she makes a mental note to fix Bertha's bun that is askew, which she does as she leans over her grandmother, who is asleep, and whispers, "Bertha, you have a visitor."

Miranda waits for Bertha's startling blue eyes to open and for her to say something like, "What the hell are you thinking, waking an old woman? Don't you know dreaming is my favorite thing to do in life? I worry that we don't dream when we die. That would be terrible, wouldn't it? To not be able to dream anymore?" But Bertha doesn't move. Miranda strokes her grandmother's arm and says, "Bertha, wake up. You have a visitor." Bertha's hand is cold. Miranda perches on the lounge and repeats, "Bertha? Bertha?"

Jonathan puts his fingers on Bertha's neck to check her pulse while checking for signs of breath that do not come. "She's gone," he says.

Miranda doesn't supress the response this time. She owes Bertha that much.

"Nothing's going to bring her back."

Back Down to Earth

Charlotte can barely see through her tears as she puts the key in the ignition and turns the engine on in the car she can no longer afford. Not after today. She uses the back of her hand to wipe away tears to scroll until she finds the song she seeks, the only song to provide solace, especially since she didn't initially pick up her phone to play music. She picked it up to call her mother, who could no longer answer, whose voice Charlotte would never hear again, causing a fresh torrent of tears. Six months and Charlotte still can't remember her mother is gone. How many times a day does Charlotte reach to text her mom? When will that instinct fade with the reality her mother is dead, her ashes spread around a tree? Charlotte knows her mother's spirit will always be with her, but her body, mind, and gentle guidance are gone forever, only to be found within the lyrics of Carly Simon's songs.

Charlotte turns up the volume to hear *Embrace Me, You Child* loudly, listening to it from beginning to end before she is empowered enough to reverse her car out of the spot in the parking garage. She winds her way into the heavy rush hour traffic to drive downtown to her apartment. Charlotte skips *Waited So Long* to hear *It Was So Easy*, singing along with gusto. Memories of following her mother through the garden, dancing in the living room, and driving in the car with the windows down flash as Carly gently sings the melancholy tune about childhood beliefs. Charlotte recites, "Step on a crack, break your mama's back," as a nod to Carly's wisdom. The singer may have been crooning about romantic love, but Charlotte's mom always made every Carly Simon song about them, like quoting lines from *The Right Thing To Do* because she always said being a mother was her life's path, her river, so to speak, and that Charlotte was as precious to her as a bouquet of flowers, as sweet as any Carly Simon song.

Mom tucked Charlotte in every night and then used Carly Simon's lyrics as taglines in their future texts as adults. But Mom isn't with Charlotte now, and for a moment Charlotte is relieved, spared the humiliation of admitting that she has failed. Fired from the job Charlotte worked years to achieve, first serving at the front desk until she had established herself worthy enough to become concierge of one of the most prestigious hotels in the city. Her mother cited *Nobody Does It Better* when Charlotte called to share the news of her promotion, making Charlotte laugh. She felt *the best* at that moment, but the magic inside her has now disappeared. What is Charlotte going to do? She is at a loss, feeling humiliated, broke, and devastated by the injustice that led to the general manager closing the door to conduct the termination meeting.

Fortunately, the funky Steely Dan-ish beat of *You Belong to Me* cues up in Charlotte's music shuffle. By the time she turns left onto her street, Charlotte is singing along, distracting herself from grief mingled with shame, compounded by the frustration of locating a space on the road to parallel park her car. No matter how often her mother encouraged her to find a better apartment now that Charlotte was earning more money as a concierge, Charlotte stood firm. Her first-floor apartment is perfect. Where else would she find her apartment's charming features, such as crystal doorknobs, original pocket doors, and fourteen-foot ceilings? Charlotte conveniently forgets the lack of central air conditioning, the wonky appliances in the kitchen, and the low water pressure in the shower installed in the claw-footed tub every time she steps out of her kitchen door into the small courtyard garden that is hers alone, privilege to the tenant on the first floor of the brownstone converted into three apartments. Directly above Charlotte lives Mrs. Parker, an old widow who rarely descends the steps, preferring to perch in her open window to watch the street below. Above Mrs. Parker, in the attic studio apartment, lives a young man named Leo, who attends art school during the day and is rarely home at night.

Charlotte's mom proposed the idea to plant a corkscrew willow in the courtyard that, in three years, has grown to provide shade over a bistro metal table and chairs where Charlotte drinks coffee on summer mornings and wine in the evenings. The brick exterior walls of the buildings enclosing the courtyard are blanketed in ivy and Virginia creeper, whose leaves turn bright red in autumn. A concrete birdbath in the far-left corner entices cardinals, wrens, and sometimes sparrows installed by a previous tenant or perhaps by the original owners of the brownstone. Charlotte plants impatiens in a ring around its base every May, the day after Mother's Day, as is the rule for planting annuals, the only flowers Charlotte plants every spring, unlike her mother, a devoted gardener. Letting go of her mother's gardens was harder than losing the actual house when Charlotte sold it last month. She can't believe she will no longer tease her mother about caring for her roses. She carefully pruned, fertilized, and spread her magic elixir of coffee grounds and eggshells as tenderly as she would care for grandchildren she dreamed of and now would never have.

Charlotte leaves the box containing her personal items from her now abandoned office at the hotel in the trunk of her car. She can deal with that later. Right now, it takes every ounce of energy she has to use her key to open the door, drop her purse on a table, and open the refrigerator to uncork the bottle of Sancerre she was saving for a special occasion. Choosing the stemless hand-blown glass her mother found at a flea market, Charlotte carries it and the bottle to her courtyard sanctuary, kicking off her high heels to walk barefoot outside. Although she cannot see the sunset, the dappled golden light reflects on the cobblestone patio Charlotte studies as she sips her first glass of wine. Before she pours a second, Charlotte retreats into her apartment to use the bathroom, then change into yoga pants and a tank top before retrieving her phone from her purse. She scrolls as she walks through the kitchen, so *Coming Around Again* plays on the outdoor speaker, tricking Charlotte into thinking she is being welcomed. To what, Charlotte isn't quite sure, only that the syncopated beats of the song are as familiar as her heartbeat, as haunting as her broken heart. Nothing may stay the same, and Charlotte was sure she was willing to play the game, but the song was pissing her off. Charlotte doesn't believe in love, and her mother had no right to be quixotic with the string of broken romances she left in her wake. Why did she teach her daughter to believe in fairy tale romances? Especially since she died alone, not in a lover's arms. Alone when the aneurysm she had carried in her brain since birth suddenly decided to explode.

As if to mock Charlotte's despondent mood, the first beats of *You're So Vain* strum. Charlotte can't help the bark of laughter that escapes. Dammit, Carly Simon. This isn't the first time Carly has betrayed Charlotte. Shame still burns the memory of third-grader Charlotte's innocent response, "Warren Beatty," to Mrs. Murphy's question, "Who can define the term *vain*?" Although the teacher was gentle, hiding a smile and responding, "Well, he is one example, I suppose," the derisive laughter of her classmates still rings in her head. Charlotte wanted to melt into her desk, she felt so embarrassed. That afternoon, Charlotte realized the lyrics of *We Have No Secrets* had nothing to do with the trust between a mother and her daughter but instead about a lover betrayed by lies. After swallowing humiliation on the yellow bus and finally entering the front door of her home, Charlotte made a beeline to the albums stacked alphabetically on a shelf in the living room. She pulled all Carly Simon's albums, carried them into her bedroom, locked the door behind her, and read the liner notes. Before the advent of the internet, that was the only way to access lyrics. Read the print on the album, something Charlotte had never done before. She had just learned to read, opening doors to the wonderful worlds of Judy Blume's stories and lifting a veil of innocence, leaving Charlotte weary of her mother, the first fissure of distrust inevitable in all mother-daughter relationships. Other than *Itsy-Bitsy Spider*, none of Carly's songs were what Charlotte's mother had her believe.

Of course, adolescence brought its avalanche of arguments stemming from power struggles between Charlotte asserting her autonomy against her mother, who anguished over her daughter's maturation journey, as evident in her mother's sentimental tears, taking pictures of Charlotte blowing out candles on her birthday cakes, Charlotte awkwardly pinning a corsage on the lapel of her prom date's tuxedo, and finally, Charlotte in cap and gown. It wasn't until Charlotte moved away to college and felt homesick did she return to the comfort of Carly Simon's songs. Charlotte forgave her mother for leading her astray with her interpretations of the songs, especially after suffering her own romantic disappointments. When Charlotte turned twenty-one, the age her mother had her, Charlotte's respect for her mother as a single parent deepened. Suddenly, the lyrics took on a dual meaning, more profound each year, until they became the soundtrack of Charlotte's life and the shorthand of her discourse with her mother.

Charlotte pours the last of the wine into her glass and scrolls until she finds the perfect song to end this terrible day. She sings with gusto, every lyric of *The Stuff That Dreams Are Made Of* slides easily off her tongue in her own backyard, not looking any further, knowing it is time to make a wish on the stars Carly Simon would shoot off.

Cosmic Charlie

The aroma of freshly brewed coffee is not enough to lift my brooding demeanor. I shuffle into the kitchen, locate my favorite mug, and pour a cup before joining my husband and our two dogs on the porch. Though it's only eight o'clock, the temperature blasts like an oven when I slide open the glass door.

"How can you be comfortable in this weather?" I grumble.

"Good morning, beautiful," my husband looks up from his phone and smiles. Typical. The man wakes up happy every day, regardless of weather, season, or aftermath of yesterday's news foretelling disaster for all American women. Shaking my head, I sip coffee and sniffle. I sit, open my mouth soundlessly, then begin to weep.

"I never thought it could happen," my husband says. "Never. It seems unbelievable to me."

I bite back, "I told you." It's not his fault. I know how he votes. It's not his fault. I love him. He's one of the good ones. It's not his fault. The one who got a vasectomy when I said *one and done*.

Maybe I was in shock yesterday, but it now settles as heavily as the humidity. I lament, "I can't stop crying. I don't even want to open my phone to read the news. I could barely sleep. I was up and down all night."

"I know," my husband says.

We sit in silence, punctuated only by our dogs' panting, bird song, and buzz of cicadas. Summer sounds that should be soothing but cannot penetrate my despair. I bite back panic and then question myself. Am I right to be alarmed, or am I overreacting? Hell, no. The Supreme Court's decision to overturn *Roe versus Wade* is terrifying. I am a human in a woman's body who cannot exercise her freedom of choice. No matter if I'm fifty-four years old, past menopause, and unable to have children anymore. I'm a woman whose country stripped her civil rights.

"And it's not going to hurt women like me," I say, switching from grief to righteous indignation. "I'm privileged. I can get an abortion as easily as I can buy a Louis Vuitton bag. This hurts impoverished women, women without resources, which means none of us are free. And it's my generation's fault. We scorned our mothers for burning their bras, and we purposefully misunderstood that a bicycle is unnecessary to a fish."

"I thought you used to protest?" my husband asks.

"I did! With a hanger around my forehead, chanting, 'Bush, stay out of mine!' but that was years ago. Years! In college."

When he stands, the dogs rise to follow. "I'm going to walk them and then run errands. Is the list on the counter ready?"

"Thank you," I say. "Wait, I'm coming in, too. I'm going to garden."

"Good idea," he says, snapping the leash on the dogs.

I retreat to the bathroom, brush my teeth, and slick my hair into a ponytail. I fill a metal tumbler with ice water in the kitchen, retrieve garden clippers from a drawer, and step into rubber boots. In my nightgown, I walk outside to the yard. I'm not the only suburban mother who gardens in her nightclothes. It's a thing.

My body is already slick with sweat when my husband returns from walking the dogs. While he runs errands, I transplant a hydrangea, remove weeds, and carefully unearth roots. Hunched over flower beds under the sweltering sun, I don't stop to help unload the car when he returns. Serves him right, I irrationally think. I've been mentally arguing with every single man on the planet. Every weed I pull, I picture an injustice. Pruning hedges, I bitterly conjure embarrassing moments because it's not enough to be angry with SCOTUS. As a woman, I shame-spiral in the process, overanalyzing every mistake I've made.

I pause to drink water, letting it run down my face and neck like a toddler, gasping between gulps. I leave the bag of trimmings behind, take caution winding the orange extension cord the way my husband prefers, and place the electric hedge trimmer on top. Before I abandon the garden, I stop to bow over scarlet begonias, willing the Grateful Dead lyrics to soothe my soul.

"I'm going to shower," I call to my husband.

Still humming the song, I visualize despair washing away as dirt swirls at the bottom of the drain. My shoulders sting under the spray, sunburned because I didn't apply sunblock. Lowering the temperature of the water, I let the cool stream rinse my body. Because I plan to wear a wraparound dress to dinner, I shave my legs and carefully moisturize.

Gazing at my reflection in the mirror, I consider the power I once enjoyed, turning heads wherever I went until I was nearly fifty and menopause ravaged my body. Suddenly, it was like I was invisible. As a feminist, an academic, an enlightened individual, I would never confess my vanity. What stupid, superficial things I obsess over. Something that should not matter but does, like picking a red dress to impress the woman of the couple we're meeting, not my husband. After twenty-two years of marriage, he says he only sees me how I looked, walking down the aisle. I choose to believe him.

At dinner, the conversation around the decision is somber, yet a relief compared to dining with some of my husband's family members who have lost their damn minds. It's almost like quarantine from the pandemic fundamentally changed society, like shock waves after an earthquake. But these dinner companions are like-minded friends, so I relax as I look around the restaurant. Rainbow-clad patrons crowd the bar, a musician plays piano, couples dine in booths, and a boisterous group dominates a long table. Driving to the restaurant, I enjoyed opening the car window to hear the Gay Pride Festival celebration downtown. Despite the heat and humidity, drag queens don their wigs, DJs turn up the tunes, and rainbow capes flow behind revelers, making me feel a bit heartened the world has not gone completely mad.

I sip wine and eat scallops and lobster ravioli as we discuss boycotting next weekend's holiday by not attending the parade, not unearthing patriotic décor, and not raising a flag. Yet, when our son returns from college, his friends will fish at our pond, so my husband will grill. That's not patriotic. That's just hospitable.

After dinner, we drive to a small venue to see live music, arriving after the band has launched first set. We make our way to the front and dance to *Sugar Magnolia*. A round stained-glass window dominates the stage's unpainted shiplap backdrop, and blue spotlights enhance a spiritual atmosphere. The band seamlessly segues into *Friend of the Devil*, and the crowd picks up the energy. I consider the Grateful Dead's lovely spirit captured by local bands around the country and how Jerry would smile in response.

A man who perhaps had *a little too much too fast* aggressively dances in my space, seeking my attention. I turn around, but my husband isn't behind me. The man continues to dance, occasionally stumbling as I smile and nod, politely turning my shoulder away from him, muttering, "It's cool. Go on, now." Before I can walk away, the intoxicated man puts his hands on my arm, my shoulder, my back. Suddenly, I hear, "Get your hands off her." I see a young man who reaches out and says,

"Seriously. Leave her alone. You need to go." Fortunately, the obnoxious man acquiesces, ambling his way back through the crowd, away from the stage. I put my hands together in prayer at my chest, smiling, and nod at the young man.

Since I now have more room, I dance while reassuring myself that I would have spoken up had that young man not interfered. Surely, I would have told the dude to fuck off, right? Or maybe I should be grateful a well-mannered young man was willing to defend a middle-aged woman, and I need to bite back resentment I know is unjustified. Why had I not walked away? As if in response, the band ends the set with *Man Smart/Woman Smarter*. The men graciously step back as women flood the front to dance the rallying cry. I'll bet they play *Throwing Stones* for encore.

At set break, I locate my husband on the patio when the young man approaches.

"Thank you," I say. "That was kind of you. What's your name?"

"Charlie," he replies. He holds up his hand to reveal a wedding band, shakes my husband's hand, and says, "I would appreciate the same if it was my wife."

"How long have you been married?" I ask.

"A year," he says, opening his phone to show me pictures of his bride.

When the band returns to the stage, my husband and I remain on the porch because I feel dizzy. I begin to sweat. I danced hard but only drank two glasses of wine at dinner, not enough to feel nauseated.

"I think I'm sick," I say to my husband, who ushers me to the car. I concentrate as we drive the few miles home. The last thing I want to do is vomit in the car or on the side of the road. Please let me make it home. I do my best not to think about the seafood. I will not consider shellfish. I know it's food poisoning. Why did I order the fish?

Fortunately, I make it home, walk upstairs, unwrap my red dress, and kneel in front of the toilet in time. I hate throwing up. I mean, who doesn't? But this time is different. For whatever reason, I want to purge. Alone, I succumb to heaving waves until there is nothing left. My husband knows better than to offer assistance. I don't want my hair held or a cool washcloth. I'm mortified. Please go away.

At the sink, I rinse my mouth, clean my face, and lie on our bed. My husband enters with a glass of water.

"Anything I can do?" he asks. "Was it the fish?"

I look at his dear face and reply, "Yes, it was the fish."

Just for Me

"Order up!" the cook barks, simultaneously ringing the bell. Kelly wipes her hands on her apron before she grabs a plate in each hand. She isn't making the same mistake twice. Although she has only worked in the diner for a week, dropping plates of food, accidentally pouring too much into a customer's cup, hot coffee overspilling onto the table, and not knowing the lyrics to the country western music is trying the nerves of the manager, Mabel. Kelly shouldn't have lied at the interview, but she needs this job. Faking it isn't working. Every time Mabel raises an eyebrow, Kelly knows Mabel is onto her. It's not like Kelly pretends to have a drawl. That would be too far, even for a liar like Kelly. She merely answers to another name printed on the tag pinned to her uniform, Rebecca, the name she provided while mumbling something about being from up north when asked where she was from. Spending her evenings on the laptop she purchased from the local pawn shop to research country music hasn't helped enough. Every time Kelly thinks she's up to speed, another song plays, and Kelly doesn't know it. Especially the old songs by dudes like Merle Haggard, Hank Williams, and Johnny Cash.

Who Kelly adores is Dolly Parton. There is something about that woman Kelly admires, surprising herself, actually. The only song Kelly knew was *9 to 5* before she landed in Kentucky. The past few days, she has spent far too many hours when she should be sleeping or doing what she should be doing following research wormholes on the country singer, who is precisely fifty years older than Kelly. The fact they share the same birthday is a sign from the Capricorn universe as far as Kelly is concerned. No matter that Dolly was born and raised in Tennessee, Kelly has never traveled south of the Mason-Dixon line and has certainly never seen the Smoky Mountains is irrelevant. They are cosmic twins. The evidence speaks for itself. Who else in the world could possibly be named Jolene? There are two Jolenes who steal men? It's so weird, Kelly wouldn't believe it, but it's true.

She is working a shitty job as a waitress, literally wearing a polyester uniform, walking across scuffed Formica floors to serve old men endless cups of coffee so they can talk all morning about the crops, pickup trucks, and town gossip, all because her husband ran off with a woman named Jolene. What are the chances? Of course, Dolly's Jolene had red hair and green eyes, and Kelly's Jolene has trampy bleached blonde with roots, not the pretty white-blond Dolly wears, but that's not the point. Nothing about the Art History degree Kelly received from Bowdoin or her two years as a docent at the Museum of Fine Arts in Boston prepared her for this work, this life, this experience. How has this happened? Kelly is only twenty-five years old. Prep school, debutant balls, and even summer camp didn't teach her survival skills. She's been running on instinct for seven days—the longest week of her life.

"Are you going to pick up those two blue plate specials, or do you expect me to do it?" Mabel asks.

"No, I've got it," Kelly says, remembering to pocket a bottle of ketchup as she delivers the plates because Mr. Simpson asks for ketchup for his meatloaf even though it's baked on top and smothered in brown gravy. Kelly tries not to look at the gelatinous mess left behind when she clears his plate, and she does almost daily. Kelly reminds herself how fortunate she is to have been born into wealth and privilege, and if she forgets, Dolly certainly reminds her with *Coat of Many Colors*. Yet, Dolly felt rich because of her mother's love, sewing patches together to surround her child with love, while Kelly's mother is so icy cold, not even the camel hair coat and cashmere sweaters Kelly own are enough to shield the chill. Still, Kelly's poverty is temporary and self-imposed. But if Dolly could climb her way out of the hills of Tennessee to become the powerhouse she is today, certainly Kelly could get it together enough to start a new life. She only has to survive. And to do that, she needs to stay hidden.

Only alone in her shitty room at the seedy motel does Kelly allow the tears to flow, listening to *I Will Always Love You*. Kelly never knew it was Dolly's song, mistakenly crediting it to Whitney Houston. So at least gaining that bit of information was valuable to Kelly, who loves trivia, constantly beating Scott by yelling the answers in questions to *Jeopardy*. No wonder Scott fell for Jolene, who looks to have the IQ of a lab rat. Wrong analogy. Lab rats are more intelligent than that stupid bitch, yet less cunning, Kelly would suppose.

The news makes Kelly freeze. There it is. What she feared. Scott filed a missing person's report and is holding a press conference, looking like a concerned husband who is terrified. Of course he's terrified. Not about where Kelly is but whether she will return. Watching his lies, she instinctually raises her hand to where her long, dark hair used to cascade to her shoulders. Reassured it is still a short pixie cut is not enough to calm her nerves. Knowing she is using the alias Rebecca, which she found out is Dolly's middle name, is yet another sign from the universe they are cosmic twins. A diner in Kentucky would be the last place Scott would ever think to look for her, which reassures Kelly for a moment until she considers her parents.

It wasn't even supposed to go on this long. Kelly wasn't thinking clearly the day she overheard Scott and Jolene's plan for her. Kelly left the museum early to surprise Scott, intending to lure him from work with a picnic at the Public Garden. She called him from the car, expecting him to be delighted to descend twenty floors in the elevator and join her in the unexpectedly mild spring weather and breathe fresh air for an hour. They would sit on the grass, eat a picnic, and maybe even have a chance to talk about the distance growing between them over the past few months. Obviously, Scott wasn't aware that his phone picked up the call when he was in his car with Jolene, and Kelly overheard their conversation. Before Kelly could say hello, she heard Jolene say, "Scott, it's not that hard. I'll do it, but it needs to be done soon so we can finally be together. Otherwise, I don't know what I'll have to do."

"It's not that easy. Poison? Are you sure? What if they trace it back to us?"

"They're not going to trace it back to us because I'm smart. Just open these two capsules and mix them into a cocktail. Not coffee. She'll taste that. Get her a little drunk, then mix the ricin in the final drink when she can't taste it. Then, we will have to lay low for a year before we can be together, so I'm telling you, the longer you wait, the longer it will take. It's the only way around the prenup."

The line disconnected as Kelly watched Scott open his car door, look around, and nod before Jolene exited the passenger seat. At first, Kelly thought the conversation, the scenario, and everything to be a joke. Undoubtedly these conspiracies for murder only happen in television shows and movies, not in real life, right? Stunned, Kelly remained in her car an hour after Scott and Jolene had entered the office building. Then she slowly drove home to pack. She unearthed an old duffel bag and tossed in jeans, t-shirts, a sweatshirt, socks, underwear, and an old cardigan sweater. Clothes that wouldn't be noticed as missing. She unearthed one credit card from her wallet and left everything else in place in her handbag she abandoned on the kitchen counter. On the bedside table, she left her cell phone and wedding band, keeping her grandmother's diamond she hung from a long gold chain she could hide in the crevice of her bra. From the back of her closet, she unearthed an old shoe box. Inside was the old fake id she used in high school, five thousand dollars cash she kept in case of emergency, and her real passport. Enough to escape.

She drove her BMW, using only cash for gas, from Boston to Cincinnati, where she abandoned the car at the airport. Using her credit card, she booked a one-way flight to Oregon. Instead of boarding the flight, she ducked into the public restroom and unearthed the kitchen scissors she was smart enough to grab and cut the credit card into tiny pieces. She flushed over and over, ensuring every shard of plastic disappeared before abandoning the scissors in the trash. Dipping into her stash of cash, Kelly purchased a burner phone to call a car to drive her to Dry Ridge, Kentucky, a place she hoped she could hide. Yet, if Scott held a press conference, they figured out Kelly wasn't on that plane to Oregon.

The Bluetooth disconnected, but Kelly couldn't believe Scott hadn't checked his call history and knew Kelly had overheard their murderous plans. Maybe he has. That's why she must remain in hiding until she can figure this out.

In hindsight, Kelly realizes she should have gone directly home to her parents. Still, assuming they would even believe her, which is highly likely they wouldn't, she imagined the look of disappointment in her father's eyes, and she couldn't make herself do it. It was bad enough when she brought Scott, an ambitious scholarship kid, home from college. Kelly should have been suspicious when Scott was so eager to sign the prenup agreement, but she was not distracted by the diamond on her finger. The diamond was a gift from her mother, the wedding ring her great-grandmother wore because Scott didn't earn enough money to buy Kelly a stone big enough for Kelly's mother's approval. She was distracted by her overwhelming love for Scott and the mind-blowing sex. Kelly had never had a boyfriend so considerate, loving, and kind. From the day they met on campus senior year, they had been inseparable, madly in love. She cried when he dropped to one knee in the courtyard on campus, proposing with a Ring Pop, making her laugh as students clapped and cheered when Scott lifted her off the ground and spun her around as they kissed. Yet, once the agreement was signed, the machine that is the Rivard Corporation, the business Kelly's father dominated, took over.

First, the engagement party, then the purchase of the house. Kelly dutifully followed her mother around Saks Fifth Avenue to register for place settings and crystal, while Scott was taken to Brooks Brothers, outfitted with six new suits, twelve white starch shirts, and twenty-four ties (Kelly counted) and then entrenched in at Rivard Co as a junior executive. Father would begrudgingly groom Scott to become the man he envisioned as son-in-law once it was evident Kelly had failed at finding a more suitable husband. Meanwhile, Mother busied herself with the elaborate details required to host a simple yet elegant wedding with no more than two hundred guests, a fraction of the size of Poppy's wedding. Typical younger sister marrying before the elder sister, Poppy was always a pain in the ass, but this attempt at sabotage, upstaging Kelly, proved fortuitous. The Rivards hosted the wedding of the season when Poppy married the right man from the country club, and the two wealthiest families rejoiced in the union. Kelly's small affair would not be held at the club but in Mother's backyard garden, where a large white tent and dance floor were rented for the occasion.

On the television, Scott looks directly at the camera and says, "I'm pleading. If anyone knows anything about my wife's whereabouts, please call. We are offering a generous reward for her safe return. Kelly, if you are watching. Honey, I love you. Come home."

Kelly snorts. Bullshit. Come home so you can kill me, maybe. No, thanks. She rises from the bed, grabs the ice bucket, some change, and the key card, and exits her room. Kelly had never stayed in a motel like this, where the door opened to a balcony wrapped around an empty courtyard below. Very retro, like in that old television show, *Melrose Place*, but without the pool. And not in California. Maybe she should move to California? Whatever she does, Kelly knows she can't go back to the diner. Hair cut or not, she would be recognized. Nobody has the bright violet eyes she has, eyes her father likened to Elizabeth Taylor, eyes Scott once equated to amethysts. In a family of blond-haired, blue-eyed people, Kelly's mother could never have expected her first-born daughter to come out with a head of dark hair and startling violet eyes that never turned brown or green but stayed violet. Of course, the family portraits reveal the family resemblances in stature, physique, and bone structure; the only difference in Kelly is her dark hair and violet eyes, a difference Kelly relished as being unique. Until now.

Settled back in her room with a full bucket of ice and a cold Sprite, Kelly pours the soda over the ice, takes a sip, and considers. She supposes that if she found an optometrist, she could be outfitted with colored contacts. Do they even make colored contacts anymore? But she can't return to the diner where Mabel has made eye contact with a woman she thinks is named Rebecca, who showed up out of nowhere and has the same unusual eye color as the picture in the press conference. Mabel may only be a diner waitress, but she isn't stupid. Time to check out of this motel and move on. Taking that job was a lark of sorts. Kelly wasn't thinking clearly the first day she woke in Dry Ridge, Kentucky, and spotted the Help Wanted sign in the corner of the diner where she ordered coffee and dry wheat toast. She applied, thinking it would keep her busy, hidden, and safe, and she was right. For seven days, Kelly was safe. She didn't account for the press conference prompting her next move, but time is of the essence.

What would Dolly do? Kelly opens her laptop and waits for the whirl of the computer to slowly hum. How she misses her MacBook. Good thing the motel is up to date enough to offer Wi-Fi, but this old laptop is driving her crazy and used up two hundred dollars she barely made up for in tips last week. Kelly created email and sock accounts for social media to scour Scott and Jolene's pages. Unfortunately, they were more privately secured than Kelly expected, which is why the press conference was such a shock. She needs to think. She needs to consider and plan. She definitely needs to check out of the motel tomorrow. She knows exactly what to do. She will purchase a car in cash and drive to California, where she will live as a woman named Rebecca. Feeling like a child the night before Christmas, Kelly is too excited to sleep. She would leave immediately, in the middle of the night, if she didn't have to wait for Duke's Auto to open.

Her entire life, Kelly followed the rules. Her only rebellious act in marrying Scott blew up in her face, and there was no way her parents would believe her. Kelly is sick of it. What she once used to soothe herself, listing the accomplishments she hoped would garner her mother's love and her father's approval, Kelly now lists as reasons to escape. Lying on her back in bed, waiting for morning, Kelly stares at the shadows on the ceiling and lists.

Years of achieving honor roll grades, scholarships to the right schools, and memberships to the right clubs yielded Kelly nothing. It does not matter that Kelly followed the rules when she donned a white gown and gloves for her debutant ball, then was accepted to her mother's alma mater and dutifully pledged to her mother's sorority. Her mother barely mumbled, "that's nice, dear," and her father merely paid the tuition and dues.

College was the first taste of freedom Kelly experienced, and look what horrible decisions she made. A worthless art history degree and marriage to a man who cheats and plans to murder her are mistakes in her past. Kelly has the right to create her future. She has no idea where in California she wants to live, having visited Los Angeles and San Francisco as a child with her family, who have no ties to the west coast. Visits to those cities were much like other trips to Manhattan, Chicago, Miami, and even Dallas her mother planned to raise her girls "well-rounded," providing anecdotes to share at cocktail parties and events. Season tickets to the traveling Broadway series, an annual pilgrimage to *The Nutcracker*, the only ballet their father tolerates, French lessons, prep school, a basic understanding between a Cabernet sauvignon and a chardonnay the lessons Kelly and her sister absorbed. Poppy embraced the lifestyle as expected, leaving Kelly disoriented in her wake.

What exactly does Kelly want with her life? What does she want to do? Tuning up *The Great Pretender*, Kelly falls to sleep to the soothing organ and Dolly's voice a few hours before she purchases a car, drives west, and becomes this new Rebecca.

A Christmas Carol

Who in the world celebrates Christmas in July? Pamela wonders as she pulls the tray of seasoned cereal mix from the oven. Of course, nobody asked Pamela to contribute, but if they were celebrating Christmas, what kind of holiday would it be without the mix? And not the store kind. The kind made with real butter, too much garlic salt, and so much Worcestershire, it darkens the cereal even before Pamela bakes it almost burned, the way her husband, Harold prefers. How do you pronounce Worcestershire? Certainly not the way Pamela's Hungarian mother taught her. So much of Pamela's language learned by a mother who spoke English as a second language was mangled anyway. Like the word *taut* is not *taunt*, yet another mistake Pamela learns, and she is in her forties and should know better. She was mortified yesterday when helping her new neighbor, Jane, string lights for this party. When Pamela said, "Pull it taunt," Jane teased, "Bad lights! Bad!"

First Jane laughed at the look of surprise Pamela couldn't conceal. Then Jane noticed Pamela's confusion and gently explained, "Taunt means to tease someone, like taunting. Taut is to pull tightly. Taut sounds like taught, the past tense of teach."

"Of course," Pamela lied, feeling embarrassed. Not only is she a mother, but Pamela is an elementary school teacher. How many other words has Pamela taught her second graders incorrectly? Does that adverb even belong at the end of the sentence?

What about Jane and her husband, Bill Manning, and their two seemingly perfect children that charm Pamela so much when she should hate them? In her casual attire of yoga pants and a plain T-shirt, Jane is more understated than most suburban moms in the neighborhood, even if the diamond studs in her ears are bigger than anyone else's. So what? Pamela has never compared herself or their possessions to anybody else. There were undoubtedly much more affluent families in their neighborhood than themselves; even though Harold's business was thriving, Pamela chose to be an educator, not a corporate woman. She knew how little teachers make and still pursued that career and has never regretted it.

There was so much to hate about Jane, who is tall, beautiful, and what's worse, thin. Jane works part-time at one of the most prestigious ad agencies in the city, dressing in high heels and looking effortlessly elegant. Nobody should be that pretty without make-up. You know, the kind of woman who can slick her hair back and look amazing while you spend hours yet will never look as good. That kind of woman. The problem is Jane is sincerely kind, thoughtful, and downright hilarious at moments, making Pamela laugh in stressful moments all moms experience, which attracts Pamela to Jane even more. It is confounding. Much easier to decide to hate the newcomer and gossip behind her back. Yet, nobody in the neighborhood has a thing to say but praise for the young family who fits in seamlessly.

Pamela calls for Snoopy, the family dog, to eat cereal she dropped on the floor before she remembers Snoopy died last month, which stings with a fresh wave of grief. What is going on with her? Irrationally irritated with Jane. Ready to burst into tears over Snoopy. Her emotions are all over the place today.

Glancing at the calendar she keeps tacked to the fridge to keep her children's activities organized, Pamela quickly calculates. She is premenstrual. Her period is due in a few days, which also accounts for the bloating. Of course, if poor Harold were ever to suggest Pamela is out of sorts because of menstruation, he would face a world of trouble, poor guy. Pamela pulls the last pan from the oven and turns it off, using a paper towel to dry the sweat on her forehead just as the kitchen door flings open, and Catherine and Cameron stomp into the house. Everything about her twins is loud, abrupt, clumsy, and oblivious as most six-year-olds.

"How was camp?" Pamela asks, offering each a small bowl of still-warm mix the children accept to take into the keeping room to watch shows before dinner, which will be eaten at the Manning's Christmas in July party tonight.

"Good," Catherine says, reaching into her backpack. "I made this in art class today. Do you like it? Miss Judy says I show promise. What does that mean, promise?"

Pamela inspects the flower her daughter carefully painted on a flat rock and replies, "In this context, it means showing promise of talent. Not like when you make a promise. Does that make sense?"

"I think it's good she promises I am talented because I am talented," Catherine says.

"And conceited," Cameron mutters, making Pamela laugh at both the wit of the remark and the fact he even knows that word. Already a voracious reader, Cameron's vocabulary promises to expand exponentially at this rate, a source of pride for Pamela and Harold. The twins' personalities were fully formed when they were born and they behaved much like the books predicted. Catherine, born ten minutes before her brother, was always loud, demanding, active, imaginative, creative, and protective of Cameron, who enjoyed the leisure of reading, video games, and lately, anime. He never cried as a baby. Didn't have to. He relied upon Catherine to voice their demands.

When Catherine took her first steps, she turned around, pulled her brother up, and held his hands for his first steps, a memory so precious to Pamela that she didn't need a video to remember. Good thing since she barely knew where her phone was in those days, feeding and chasing toddlers between endless diaper changes. Only Harold knows what a relief it was when the twins turned three, and Pamela felt comfortable enough to put them in daycare so she could return to teaching. The mothers in their neighborhood claim to love staying home with their children, anguishing over their first days of preschool, a mere four hours an eternity to the mothers separated from their precious children. On the first day, there is always a tea in the school library so the mothers can weep together. Weep and exchange contact information, trustworthy babysitters' names, the newest yoga classes, and the best pedicure spots—mother networking at its finest.

There is a difference between being a teacher in a second-grade classroom and being a mother to infants and toddlers, in Pamela's experience. It isn't as if she doesn't adore Catherine and Cameron, but Pamela's first three years of their lives were a blur of exhaustion while Harold steadily built his business. The freedom Pamela felt when she turned up the radio and opened the window in her car after dropping her newly potty-trained children at daycare to drive the few miles to the elementary school to teach her class was exhilarating. Pamela sang along with Katy Perry, mumbling over the lyrics she didn't know, which were more than she did know, until the refrain. Pamela likes how Katy breaks the word *roar* into two syllables.

She checks on her children, settled in the keeping room, television blasting, so Catherine can sing her daily dissent to Bruno while Cameron's nose is in a book.

"I'm going to take a shower and dress. We're going to the Manning's Christmas in July party tonight," Pamela says. "I've set outfits on your beds. Please wash your faces and change before Dad arrives home, so we're ready, okay?"

Cameron nods, and Catherine replies, "Christmas in July! Awesome, Mama. Is Santa coming? We'll be ready. Do we get presents?"

Pamela replies as she does in December. "If you're good. He's watching," and turns to walk the hallway to her bedroom. She has no idea if Santa is making an appearance at the party. She has no idea what to expect. It's her first Christmas in July party, too.

When her family rings the Manning's doorbell, Pamela is proud. The full skirt of her red sundress hides her premenstrual pooch, and looks cute next to Harold, good-naturedly wearing the green polo shirt Pamela set out for him. The twins are dressed in white polos and red shorts. Pamela wove a green ribbon in the belt loops of Catherine's shorts and crisscrossed new green laces into Cameron's sneakers for an extra festive touch.

Jane and Bill open the door and greet them, accepting the container of snack mix Pamela awkwardly offers. Behind them, from inside the house, the sound of Christmas carols, not from a recording but from an actual group of carolers dressed in Victorian costumes.

"It wasn't easy finding a choir this time of year, but I was determined," Jane says as she escorts them into the house decorated as if it is truly December. Pine boughs around every doorway, poinsettias in abundance, even a fully decorated Christmas tree and stockings on the mantle. It exhausts Pamela to look at it.

"I know! I know!" Jane exclaims as if Pamela has spoken.

Jane turns to the twins and says, "The kids are out back, decorating gingerbread houses," before turning to Pamela and asking, "Drink?"

"Please," Pamela replies, following Jane into the kitchen, stopping to greet neighbors on the way. She spots Harold in the corner, chatting with Mr. Bernstein, an elderly widower living on their street. The two men share a passion for baseball and are probably discussing the Red's epic loss the other night.

Jane pulls a bottle of champagne from the wine fridge and nods to the flutes lined up on the marble counter of the expansive island in the kitchen. The women clink glasses before they sip.

"I know this is absolute madness, but after boycotting the Fourth of July, the summer seemed to stretch on endlessly, and this was all I could come up with," Jane says.

"You boycotted Fourth of July?" Pamela asks.

"After the Supreme Court overturned *Roe versus Wade*? You didn't? We were going to participate in the parade and everything. You know, decorating their bicycles with crepe paper and little flags I secretly burned in the backyard when nobody was looking." When Pamela's eyes widen, Jane says, "Shh! That's our secret. Anyway, my kids still haven't forgiven me. Hence …" Jane waves her hand for emphasis. "They're too little to understand now, but I'm raising little women, for fuck's sake. They'll appreciate it in the future, and in the meanwhile, bribery will get you everywhere."

Pamela bursts out laughing. It doesn't matter how gorgeous Jane looks in an unforgiving dress, how perfectly groomed her handsome husband is, or the elaborate party in their beautiful home. The words that come from Jane's mouth are outrageous, delighting Pamela. This is why she likes her new friend so much. This.

Pamela follows Jane to the backyard, where the children happily decorate gingerbread houses, stuffing as much candy into their mouths as they glue with icing. Before Pamela can ask, Jane says, "Amazon. Fucking Amazon has everything, right?"

They join the adults gathered on the other side of the patio. A long table covered in linen supports silver trays of appetizers interspersed with silver-fluted vases filled with red and white geraniums. Pamela fills a plate with mini quiche, asparagus spears wrapped in prosciutto, vegetables she will not eat, and exactly three crackers smeared with cheese before adding four shrimp. Harold approaches and helps himself to one of the crackers as Pamela chats with their neighbors. She whispers, "I squeezed lemon for you," as he munches on the shrimp.

The children are ushered into the house for their dinner of macaroni and cheese, hot dogs, carrots, and Ranch dressing they will plate to take into the basement recreation room to watch *Polar Express* so the parents can eat under the canopy of lights Pamela helped Jane string yesterday. Servers sporting Santa hats hustle to exchange the appetizer trays with chafing dishes so the guests can help themselves to lemon chicken, salmon, or roast beef carved by a man in a white chef hat. The sun sets as the guests eat and drink. Pamela wonders where the carolers have gone and is secretly relieved for the moment's silence. The only other sounds than dinner conversation are the chirp of crickets and cicadas, reassuring Pamela of the season in this otherwise disorienting dinner party. She is distracted from studying lightning bugs in the trees at the edge of the yard by the return of the children to the backyard.

Catherine and Cameron run to their parents, each holding a stocking. "Look, Mom! Look, Dad! This is the best party ever!" Catherine exclaims.

Everyone turns and silences at the clank of a knife against a wine glass held by Jane, who says, "Thank you, everyone! We so appreciate you indulging our Christmas in July. We hope you have enjoyed the food and each other. Moving here was the best thing we ever did." The guests applaud in response. Jane smiles as her husband puts his arm around her waist. "This one's for you, honey," Jane says, setting her champagne flute on a table as a song cues up on outdoor speakers. The minute Pamela hears Laura Nyro's unmistakable lament, "Bill," in the song *Wedding Bell Blues*, a mixture of laughter and tears bubble as Pamela watches how elegantly the Mannings dance to what is obviously *their* song. At the second refrain, Jane addresses her guests with laughter, "Come on, everyone. Please join us."

When Harold looks at Pamela, she says, "It's time to go. We need to get these two in bed." He raises an eyebrow but doesn't protest, knowing it's the last thing she will tolerate in the face of their children's whining when they are told it is time to leave the party. Pamela catches Jane's attention as they usher the twins through the backyard gate and mouths, "Thank you." Jane winks in response as her husband spins her around the dance floor to Ella Fitzgerald singing *Let's Do It (Let's Fall in Love)*. Impossibly romantic, exactly why she hates Jane so much.

Take Five

Paige cues up Dave Brubeck's Quartet and inserts the tiny white buds into her ears to launch her daily walk. The only good thing to come out of this era is the ability to stream music. Now Paige can actually hear the soundtrack of her life and not just through memory. The music inspires her to follow her cardiologist's dire warnings. Anything to stay out of the doctor's office, and if a daily walk does the trick, Paige asked her favorite grandson to help her curate different playlists so she would have no excuse not to do her cardio or whatever nonsense her daughter calls it. Paige calls it a walk. All New Yorkers walk.

Paige doesn't know exactly when in childhood this habit of mentally streaming music started. She only knows there is a song for every moment of her waking life. And sometimes in her dreams, too. You would assume Paige is a musician; she loves music so passionately, but alas, after months of tedious piano lessons, it was quite apparent that six-year-old Paige lacked that certain something musicians must possess to play the most rudimentary melodies, and she did it badly. It made no difference to Paige, who would rather listen to music than make it, even though learning to play clarinet in what is now called middle school was a heady experience once the band accomplished playing an entire song. She doesn't regret abandoning the woodwind in high school in lieu of pursuing a romance with Joe. He proved to be a good husband and a wonderful father. Not to mention the perfect lover.

Not that Paige would have anyone else to compare to Joe. When they married in 1965, it wasn't unusual for a woman to be a virgin. Paige surrendered to Joe when they became engaged, grateful for the birth control pill, regardless of the Supreme Court's recent decision, *Griswold versus Connecticut*. Nobody paid any attention to it anyway. And Paige was lucky. No unwanted pregnancies for her, no scandals, nothing but the soundtrack of her life she cues up mentally. Until now. Now, she has the real thing. Any song, anytime, anywhere Paige happens to be.

Jazz is the perfect music for walking the same streets she has walked her entire life. Paige purposefully turns to avoid where Walden School used to be because the weather is too pretty to be depressed. Both Paige and Joe attended Walden, even though their children attended Stuyvesant, of course. Long gone are the days of intellectualism and progressive innovations in education found at Walden. Both her children were more concerned with test scores and advanced placement credit anyway.

Paige spent her childhood and then raised her family in the same apartment. To Joe's credit, he supported and cared for Paige's parents, who lived with them once he reluctantly agreed to move into the Eldorado after the wedding. Of course, it wasn't unusual back then for extended families to live together. Paige snorts laughter when she considers living with either of her grown children and their families. Fat chance, even if they offered, which would never occur to either of them, busy working, sustaining marriages while raising their children. It's enough that Paige travels once a year to each child's home, one in Cleveland, the other in Topeka, to spend a week with her grandchildren, whom Paige adores. Paige doesn't ask why her children choose such boring places to live. She knows the answer: work, always work. A week in the suburbs is enough to spur Paige back to the city she adores to live in the same apartment she has inhabited for almost seventy-five years.

Their building is located on Central Park West in Manhattan called the Eldorado, a bit less pretentious than the Dakota and 88 Park West, but there have been some celebrities who have lived in the building over the years, like the new red-headed fellow who plays with some band and likes to walk when he is not touring. Paige can never remember his name when they pass each other in the marble lobby or happen to be riding in an elevator together, but she appreciates his good manners. Once, she spotted a lipstick stain on his cheek, reminding Paige of her habit of kissing Joe purposefully whenever he went out, leaving a trace of lipstick like a mark. Silly, sentimental moments wove the fabric of a life they built together for forty years until Paige was widowed five years ago. Or is it six?

Their apartment has eight rooms and three bathrooms (if you count the powder room, which Paige does). It features a wood-burning fireplace and windows overlooking the Jacqueline Kennedy Onassis Reservoir. The art deco design of the building never ceases to delight Paige, who always slows her pace in the lobby. Although she has never been to the basement exercise room, there is nowhere else she would rather live.

Paige loves gazing at the reservoir from the windows of their twenty-fourth-floor apartment, appreciating being lucky enough to live in one of the towers. Her mother liked to watch for herons, believing the birds brought luck. Paige's father said it was because his wife grew up in Kentucky that she yearned for nature, living in one of the biggest cities in the world with only Central Park as a respite to her country soul.

"Don't try to analyze me. Stick to your clients and leave me be," her mother would say, referring to her husband's patients. Paige's father was a psychotherapist who claimed one of the large bedrooms as an office, outfitting it with special soundproofing for the walls and door. Still, Paige grew up with her mother constantly saying, "Shh! Your father has a patient. Be quiet," inspiring Paige to cue up *My Little Brown Book* by Duke Ellington for the memory as she walks the last blocks to reach Steinem's, one of the last family-owned delis in the neighborhood. Of course, it's Mr. Steinem's son, Lyle, who now runs the store, but they still make the matzo ball soup the same, which is good since Paige eats it several times a week for dinner now that she no longer cooks as she used to when raising her family. Why bother cooking for one? It was hard enough to learn to cook for two when the children left for college, and Paige hates to waste food.

Paige has manners enough to remove her buds when she carries her items to the counter, the white container of hot matzo ball soup prepared and ready for her by Lyle, who exchanges pleasantries with her as they do almost every day. Nothing too personal even though their relationship has lasted longer than most, but it's like that in New York when you actually live in the city and not commute to Long Island or New Jersey every day. Paige asks the bodega owner about his son's baseball career but doesn't even know if he is married or has other children. She and the same woman who walks her aging beagle to the same bench in the park discuss the weather. Even a city large as Manhattan becomes a small neighborhood in its familiarity. People are habitual by nature, Paige's father would say.

Paige scrolls to find *A Moment's Notice* because John Coltrane is her favorite. She and Joe loved the Village Vanguard, especially in the early seventies. Descending into the damp basement always promised something special, delivering the likes of Art Pepper, Miles Davis, and even Thelonious Monk. While her mother would feed the children dinner, Paige would take advantage of the babysitting to linger in a bubble bath before using extra care with her hair and dress to remind Joe a sexy woman still existed underneath her daily maternal demeanor. She nearly groans as she remembers what kept them up until dawn. There are many things she misses about Joe. Sex probably the most, a thought a seventy-four-year-old woman would never confess aloud, as if geriatric women are incapable of sexual desire. For the record, nobody is too old for an orgasm.

Nothing to cue up but Billie Holiday in response to the longing in Paige's heart. She can still taste Joe at the back of her throat. Although Billie yearns for *April in Paris*, Paige will take New York in any season but agrees. *This is a feeling/No one can ever reprise.*

The Core

When the spotlights shine from behind, Grover looks like an angel, something Emily never tires of watching. Mesmerized with his shaggy hair obscuring romantic brown eyes, Emily fell in love with him the moment she first saw him on stage two months ago. Okay, well, maybe not love exactly, but she is definitely obsessed. Emily wasn't even planning to go out, and only gave in to her roommate, Rochelle's persistence because otherwise, Emily would be stuck scrolling endless internet videos with Rochelle, who needs constant entertainment. And because the promise of backstage passes Rochelle dangled were too good an opportunity for Emily to miss. Choosing to passively watch a band on stage seemed the easiest, if not laziest option, if Emily can quell the butterflies of anticipation. After ordering from the bar, Rochelle drags Emily down the aisle to third row just as Grover and the other band members take the stage. Suddenly, Emily doesn't feel tired anymore.

Tonight, at set break, they will finally meet. Emily smiles, feeling a bit like a sixth-grader who has just found out the boy you like likes you back because he told his friend who told your friend and maybe there was a note written in pencil on lined paper folded into a triangle that could also be used as a football the boys played with on their desks in the classrooms and at the tables in the cafeteria. The familiar jitters cause her heart to flutter and mingle with the maturity of adult desire that wasn't even an idea in sixth grade. At least not for Emily, who didn't even have her first real kiss until the summer between seventh and eighth grade in the woods at Camp Fitch with a boy they called Matt from New Jersey. Emily still has a box containing the letters she and Matt exchanged in September, dwindling off by November, when summer camp became nothing more than a fond memory and also because Harrison, the boy who played first chair saxophone had garnered her attention from her place as second chair flutist. Emily distinctly remembers because it was the last year she played with the school band before she devoted herself in earnest to the piano, dedicating every spare moment of her life until she was accepted to the music conservatory of her choice and met her dorm roommate, an English major named Rochelle. The two became fast friends, choosing to rent an apartment together this year.

In fifteen minutes, Grover would no longer be Grover. Not the Grover Emily imagines in her fantasies. Instead, he will become a real person. Emily tugs Rochelle's sleeve and yells, "I'm running to the restroom."

Rochelle replies, "I'll come with you."

Emily touches her backstage pass dangling around her neck and smiles as the friends make their way through the dancing crowd to the restrooms. Luckily, there isn't a line, so the two are able to use the stalls before meeting at the sinks, making eye contact through the mirrors as they wash their hands, and Emily reapplies lipstick.

"This is going to be good. I've been to their apartment. Hung out with them all. I think Grover and Joe went to high school together. I'm not sure when they met Brandon and Kyle," Rochelle says, referring to the band members who rent a house together off campus a few blocks away from the girls' apartment building. "But I know they've been playing together as a band for at least a year now. Did you see the crowd? It's the biggest I've seen yet, don't you think? They'll be psyched at set break. It's perfect. Relax."

Emily follows Rochelle, who confidently leads them into the backstage area past a surprisingly wimpy-looking security guard by raising her pass, as the band finishes their set. Over applause and cheers, Emily hears Joe say into the microphone, "Thank you. We'll be right back for a second set," because Joe is the lead guitarist, lead vocalist, and the one to engage with the audience the most.

Emily accepts a bottle of water from Rochelle, who helped herself from a tub full of ice and drinks and then leads Emily to chairs against a red brick wall as the band files in, chattering and laughing. Emily watches as Kyle kisses his girlfriend and Brandon shakes hands with an older man while Grover and Joe are bowed over in conversation. When Grover meets Emily's eyes, smiles, and after patting Joe on the back, approaches her, she realizes the two months she fantasized about this man is the same time she fantasized about Matt from New Jersey. Of course, these aren't the only two men Emily has woven entire romances with in her own imagination, if you counted the golfer in high school who looked gorgeous in his polo shirts, the lifeguard at the pool who had a perfect tan and a crooked smile, and a certain TA in her dorm freshman year who Emily hooked up with, much to her consternation. It was terrible. A complete disappointment from what she expected.

"Hey, Rochelle," Grover says. Then he turns to Emily and says, "Hi. I'm Grover."

"Hi, Grover. I'm Emily," she says and then can't think of a single thing to say.

"Emily the pianist I have been telling you about," Rochelle says. "She's wicked talented."

Grover smiles. "Where do you play?"

"Wherever I can, I guess," Emily says. "But mostly at school. With the symphony. Not with a band like yours or anything. I study classical piano."

"Don't let her fool you. She's a music prodigy in the college conservatory of music but excuse me, please. I'm going to say hello to Joe," Rochelle says, walking away, attempting to give Emily a subtle wink Grover catches and grins.

"I hope you liked first set," Grover says. "I screwed up on *Hero*. Did you hear? I think I recovered enough, but I'm sure you probably noticed. I mean, maybe you don't know our songs very well so you couldn't notice, but still. I felt like an asshole. I mean, I know musicians don't hit every note every time, but still …"

"I didn't notice a thing, and *Hero* is one of my favorite songs. Did you write it?"

"Yes. I mean, most of the songs, Joe writes, you know? But *Hero* just kind of came to me one day," Grover says, looking quietly pleased. Emily can't believe he is as sincere, shy, and mostly as vulnerable as he is, admitting his mistake to her. She realizes he is waiting for her to say something, but again, for whatever reason, her mind is completely blank. Like, there isn't a single solitary thing she can think to say.

"Well, I see you got a water. Is there anything else I can get you?"

When Emily shakes her head no, he asks, "May I sit with you for a moment?"

"Of course," Emily says.

"What is your favorite music to play?" Grover asks.

"I study classical at school, of course, but I love jazz, rock and roll, and rhythm and blues. That's my secret, though. My teacher isn't training me to be a pop star, so I don't get much time to play what I want to play."

"What is your teacher training you for?"

"To join a professional symphony after college or get picked up by a talent agent and become famous, or in the worst-case scenario, play in a hotel lobby, I guess."

Grover laughed. "I don't think this bar is much better than playing in a hotel lobby. I mean, look at this," he says, gesturing to the dingy backstage space filled with the band members and girls drinking from red solo cups. The courtesy table features an open box of stale donuts, a bag of potato chips, and bottles of water everyone bypasses for a swig from the handle of whiskey instead.

"I would love to hear you play sometime. May I call you?" Grover asks as he stands. There are only a few moments remaining before the band needs to take the stage to finish the show, so Emily quickly enters her number into his phone. Later, when Grover texts her, she replies, *Practice Room 555* and is not surprised when she hears a knock Monday afternoon and finds Grover standing at the doorway, guitar in hand.

"Good," Emily says, waving Grover into the small space. "If I have to suffer through one more Mozart concerto, I'm going to lose my mind."

"One more time?" Grover asks. He sits on a chair, sets his guitar case on the floor, and turns to Emily. "Would you play something for me?"

Emily launches with Bach's Keyboard Concerto No. 5 before playfully segueing into Mozart's Piano Sonata No. 11 in A Major. Suddenly, she switches gears, looks directly at Grover, and smiles as he recognizes the first notes of *Philosophy* by Ben Folds Five. When she opens her mouth to sing, his mouth gapes in surprise. By the time she reaches the chorus, Grover is singing with her, both of them harmonizing with gusto as if they have been singing together forever.

"Ben Folds?" Grover asks when they finish laughing at the end of the duet.

"Of course. Ben Folds, Marco Benevento, Jeff Chimenti, and I can't forget the Chairman of the Board, Page McConnell. My favorite pianists, other than Lang Lang, Martha Argerich, and Yuja Wang, of course. But there's something about how Ben bangs the piano that gets me."

"Will you sing me another song, please?" Grover says, reaching to retrieve his guitar from its case. "Then I will play for you. I have an idea."

"What do you want to hear?" Emily asks, but before he can respond, begins *If I Ain't Got You* by Alicia Keys. When Grover nods at the end of the song, Emily tosses her hair behind her shoulders and quietly begins *Certainly* by Erykah Badu.

"Well, I have no interest in rearranging you or fixing you, but I would love to sing with you," Grover says in response.

"What exactly is a mickey?" Emily asks.

"I think it's an old-fashioned word for being roofied. The date rape drug, Rohypnol maybe?"

"That's crazy! I had no idea that song was about rape. I'm never playing it again," Emily says, feeling almost betrayed by this information. And she loves Erykah Badu.

"Well, maybe you'll like this one better. Have you ever heard this song?" Grover says. Emily bursts into tears as Grover strums the first chords of Eric Clapton's song, *The Core*.

"What's wrong? You hate this song? Emily, what is it?" Grover says, alarmed at her reaction.

"How did you know?" Emily manages to ask as she reaches in her backpack for a tissue. Of course, there are no tissues in the bag, but Emily locates a napkin left over from her breakfast muffin to wipe her tears. She takes a deep breath, tilts her head, and gazes at Grover, who looks so concerned, she rushes to reassure him. "I love this song. I'm ready. Start again."

Grover pauses, then nods. He begins the song and lights up when Emily doesn't hesitate to sing the first verse Marcy Levy sang with Clapton. Grover responds with the next verse as Emily grins. Together, their voices blend at the chorus, and Emily's fingers dance across the keys, joining Grover's guitar.

"You know Marcy Levy co-wrote *Lay Down Sally* with Clapton, right?" Emily says.

"Emily, I didn't even know Marcy Levy's name until just now. I just know the song," Grover says.

"My dad was a huge Clapton fan. He taught me all his songs." Before Grover can respond, Emily jumps up and says, "Look at the time. I've got class."

Although there is clearly no clock in the practice room, nor is Emily's phone in sight, Grover understands he has inadvertently stepped into something and takes her cue by packing his guitar into its case and following her out of the room. In the hallway, he says, "Hey, I didn't mean to—" just as Emily says, "I'm sorry if I seem weird—" which makes them laugh.

"Don't worry about it. I'll call you, okay?" Grover says.

"I'd like that," Emily says. They exit the building and walk in separate directions on campus.

A few weeks later, Emily and Rochelle hustle to choose the perfect outfit for Emily to wear on stage, discarding this top and those pants until the friends agree what looks best. Sexy enough for Rochelle and comfortable enough for Emily.

Rochelle gazes into her friend's eyes through the mirror and asks, "You're going to do it, right?" She holds up the curling iron as if it's a microphone and starts singing off-key until Emily laughingly takes the iron and says, "Yes, yes. But only if you can get my hair right."

Rochelle says, "Relax, I've got you. I can't believe you're nervous. I've never seen you nervous before a performance with the orchestra or your recitals or anything really."

"This is different. I'm singing," Emily says. "And I can't even hide behind a piano. I have to, like, stand there. At the mic. In front of everyone."

"You know your dad would be so proud of you, Em," Rochelle says as she finishes the last curls of Emily's hair. "Now close your eyes and mouth because I'm going to spray your hair until it's lacquered."

Emily puts her hand up in protest. "Not too much."

"Relax," Rochelle says. "We just want the curls to stay in place."

As Emily closes her eyes, she pictures her father's face. It's so comforting, she does the same thing the moment the band plays the last notes of *Hero*, Emily's cue to join Grover on stage. She's glad to have chosen to wear jeans because her legs are shaking so much, she has to stamp her foot to stop the nerves. Grover smiles reassuringly as he addresses the audience.

"Hey there! I want to introduce you to my friend, Emily. Can you give it up for Emily?" Grover says as the audience cheers and applauds. "She's going to sing a song with me. You guys want to hear a Phish tune?"

Because the band rarely covers songs, choosing to play their own music as much as possible, the crowd roars in response. Not to mention, in the jamband community, Phish is highly regarded, so Emily is greeted with the warmth Grover assured her when he asked her to sing the song *If I Could* with him. Joe begins the song as Grover and Emily share a mic and sing the first verse in unison. By the second verse, Emily feels comfortable enough to sing her lyrics and can't stop the grin when Grover responds with his. Together, their voices soar, and by the end, Emily feels so invigorated, she is swaying and dancing on stage. In front of everyone. But it feels so good when the audience sings along, and the band is in synch, and everything's right in the universe under the lights on a stage. The song may end with the phrase, *but I don't know how,* but Emily disagrees.

What's Love?

It is the famous lobby scene that shocks me the most. Not the violence in the limo. Not the blood, cuts, and bruises inflicted between husband and wife. The idea that Tina and Ike Turner just saunter into a swanky hotel without a backward glance. Well, okay, cobble into the lobby better describes it. The public spectacle is what upsets me to my core.

That's not how beatings go down in my house. And I've certainly never fought back like Tina did in that limo. When I think of the money I've invested in the heavy theater makeup to cover bruises, the lies told as excuses to not attend events, the bright façade of a happy family we portray in our neighborhood, that scene in the Tina Turner movie acts as a serious wake-up call. Not just for Tina, who left Ike after that. For me.

What do I do? Leave my husband, abandon the house, report the abuse? Of course not. I'm Mrs. Richard Zale. It's just not done in our world. Instead, I will learn to meditate. What is the phrase Tina repeats? A quick scroll on the internet hooks me up with video tutorials Tina has created to teach us. What can't this woman accomplish? Domestic violence survivor, famous singer, triumphant rock star, now spiritual guru? Okay. Chanting Oprah's ah-ha moments didn't get me far. I'm with Tina.

Not that I would ever leave Richard. That's not the point. I'm seeking a better way to handle what I call my parallel universes. It's like I live two truths at the same time, always looking to reconcile how one truth is so far from the other. Like a princess locked in the tower of a castle, our home serves as such for me, yet it has been featured in architectural and interior design magazines, and therefore, what should be a private home has been on display for all the world to see. Well, at least the people in the world who read such magazines happen to be the kind of people Richard cares about. As a family, we are always on display. Richard is a wonderful provider and the best father. Our children seek his approval much as flowers tilt their faces to the sun, and he rewards them with his golden beam, proving to me he has a pure heart. How can he be a monster when he's been so good to our children? He has never even so much as spanked them when they were toddlers, and he always takes care to contain his violence behind the privacy of our bedroom door and of course, only unleashes on me because really, I deserve it. Not them. Our children are perfect. It's me. And we are known as the yummy couple, a label I despise, but it's true.

Even into our early fifties, Richard and I look good together. I know that sounds vain, but trust me, I put no value into the façade we present. I know the truth. Even a lapsed Catholic still mumbles prayers to a rosary, only instead, I recite each beating by counting not beads that end in a cross, but by counting baubles in my jewelry box, listening to Tina sing *The Best*. Not sure how *simply the best* is, but I like the sentiment. I lift the ruby ring haloed in diamonds Richard gifted me after breaking two of my ribs and study the tennis bracelet crafted with so many carats it weighs down my wrist. Intended as distraction from six stitches (stupid of me to run into a door, I tell the emergency room nurses. And Richard is usually so careful about my face). Then, I palm the sapphire earrings Richard insists I wear to the country club because he spent a fortune on them and wants everyone to know it. That gift was offered to make up for a beating so bad, I've blacked it out. I try not to look at the Cartier bangle permanently locked to my wrist. I'm sure Richard doesn't even remember where he hid the key, and I've never searched. It takes everything I have to pull the instinctual grimace into a gracious smile every time a (usually younger) woman sighs how romantic that bracelet is. I take a sip of champagne or pretend to sneeze to muffle the guffaw I want to explode. There is nothing romantic about shackles. That *Fifty Shades* writer can titillate the suburban world with her erotic bondage. She obviously has never met a man like Richard, and from what I assume, has enough of her own money to tell any man to fuck off. Not me. I have absolutely no resources, too stupid to create secret accounts, and really, haven't been trained to do anything other than be a corporate wife, so what kind of work do I think I could get, even if I were brave enough to try? My fine arts degree in painting serves only as excellent cocktail party banter. Besides, it's been almost five months in this honeymoon phase. As long as I continue to tiptoe and not trigger Richard, maybe I'll be safe? After thirty years of marriage, maybe he will finally wind down like a toy with low batteries.

First, I need an altar. I zoom to study hers as a model before I decide the best place for me to create a sacred space is where Richard would never think to wander. The pantry inside the kitchen is the most obvious secret place, but I don't trust Mrs. Murdock, our housekeeper. She has betrayed me to Richard in the past, and she won't bat an eyelash to do it again. Only the fact that I can't imitate her beef Wellington recipe (and I've tried. Trust me, I've tried) stops me from firing her. There has to be somewhere secret in this house, for God's sake. Seven thousand square feet on three acres. I just need to think. Meanwhile, what do I need to purchase for this altar and new meditation practice? Surely a humungous Buddha statue is too conspicuous to pass Mrs. Murdock's notice as she is the one to accept deliveries. It occurs to me how strange the idea to drive to an actual store to shop is to me in the post-quarantine world. Even a year after rounds of boosters isn't enough to welcome me back into the general public on the same level I used to. And it's not fear of the virus that inhibits me. It's people. Crowds.

The first time I went to a department store, the only place I can find Manolo Blahniks, it was odors that assaulted my senses. Perfume, shampoo, cologne, sweat masked by deodorant. Human smells I hadn't encountered in almost two years overwhelmed me, causing me to abandon the perfect slingbacks, grab my Neverfull, and hustle out of the store, back to the safety of my Mercedes. I cued up *River Deep-Mountain High* to drive home because back then, I was still committed to being loyal as our family dog. Was Tina singing this song to convince herself to stay with Ike? I know that's what was in my heart as I sang at the top of my lungs, mumbling the lyrics I'd yet to memorize. I remembered the song from my childhood. It wasn't unfamiliar, but I never knew the spirit of Tina could save my life. I didn't know a lot of things back then, but I'm getting ahead of myself.

Children are saviors, or maybe that's how they've operated in my life, casting me into role of Mother, which does garner some level of respect, if not complete safety. I will admit, Richard never raised a hand to me those early days when I was breast-feeding and chasing toddlers. For a few sweet years, I felt the Madonna I was. It wasn't until the children were old enough to go to school, which coincided with Richard's promotion, rocketing him up the corporation at lightning speed, did the pressures intensify enough for him to explode, and really, the first strikes weren't even that bad. A slap across the face, a push into the wall, and a lot of temper tantrum destruction of objects, which in hindsight, weren't as painful as the escalating violence on my body. But I digress.

The point I'm making is if my daughter hadn't insisted on the exact trunk she lugged to summer camp every year to take with her to her first apartment off-campus, I would never be compelled to climb the attic stairs. Especially not in late August when the sweltering heat of the unfinished space is unbearable. I feel a pang of regret realizing what Mrs. Murdock suffers every season when I instruct her to retrieve the autumn décor totes, never once considering her discomfort. Although the attic is unfinished, beams exposed, no central air and heating system, floors rough planks, it is meticulously organized, as is every space in this house. Labeled totes line the walls, clothing racks protected with heavy quilted coverings keep the ballgowns and cocktail dresses I've worn to events over the years. I never wear the same dress twice but can't bear to part with them. Again, I feel the tug of Catholic guilt. I should donate these clothes. It's a sin for them to languish, unused. I spy the empty trunk and push it easily across the floor, then pause.

How had I ever forgotten my original plans for this attic space? I flash back to the day Richard and I climbed these stairs, our realtor waiting for us in the foyer.

"And this will be your studio. Someday we'll finish this space, but look, honey," he said, pointing to the floor-to-ceiling Palladio window that faced the front of the house. "All the natural light you'll need. That's what you're always saying, right? Natural light?"

I smiled but was too distracted with my concern of how I was going to climb back down those stairs, seven months pregnant. I wanted to look at the room I imagined would be the nursery again. Two children, three dogs, and twenty years later, I never once did anything with this space but use it as storage. That was going to change.

Unbeknownst to my family, the day we waved and bid our youngest child farewell, her car packed, every inch full, I had already hired an entire crew to begin my secret project. Our son had left the week before to prepare for fraternity rush, and miraculously, Richard's travel agenda suited my schedule. Moments after his driver sped Richard away to the airport, the workers I hired arrived. In one day, they successfully emptied the attic for me. Totes I wanted to keep were lugged all the way down to the basement, where there was ample space in yet another storage room in this house. Of course, there is space. In a house this big, I have bathrooms that remain unused for months, yet insist Mrs. Murdock sanitize every week, ready for unexpected guests who never arrive. Two volunteers from church arrive to accept the clothing donation. Mrs. Murdock raises an eyebrow during the chaotic eight hours but knows better than to ask questions.

In the newly furnished yet-to-be-decorated attic space, I carry a candle, a bottle of chardonnay, my favorite Baccarat crystal wineglass, and climb the stairs. Through the window, the moon hovers at the exact right spot in the sky to cast its glow on the floorboards. I sit cross-legged on the floor, pour a glass of wine, light the candle, and raise the glass. I pause, unsure what to toast. Perhaps I should pray, considering this wine as sacrament. Or maybe I should just get good and drunk, a luxury I never allow myself. Richard's two glass rule applies not just to himself, but to me. Not tonight, buddy.

I toast the workers who were so strong, they appeared to be carrying empty boxes and plastic furniture up and down the flights of stairs until I was satisfied the job was completed, tipping them extravagantly after paying the invoice. The movers carried a long wood table that languished in the basement to the attic and placed it under the window where I plan to work. In the left corner, I positioned an end table from one of the many unused guestrooms to serve as an altar. I plan to drape it with a tapestry Richard haggled in a Turkish market in Istanbul because I like the stars and moons embroidered in the fabric even though it has never left the top of the linen closet because its jewel tones clash against the décor of the house. From the china cabinet in the dining room, I chose several candlesticks, crystal, sterling silver, wood I plan to place on the altar along with a picture of Tina I framed. Instead of a Buddhist statue, one of my favorite garden gnomes will anchor the altar. I've collected a few gnomes and have even created fairy gardens when the children were little and enchanted by such magical realities. I welcome the gnome's friendly presence and trigger for such nostalgia as I move into the future, manifesting the dreams I will weave into a reality beyond what I can imagine.

This will be my space. I will retreat from the rest of the house to this attic. Here, I will meditate, make art again, purchase an easel, brushes, and paints. I will claim the dream I once had of being an artist and not just Richard's wife and our children's mother. I think about the scene in the movie where the music executive questions Tina's decision to break into the rock and roll scene at such an old age, her mid-forties. If she could become famous at that age, I can, at least, make art at mine. I harbor no fantasies about becoming rich and famous. I just want to express myself and do things that please me. I deserve that, don't I? The children are in college. The family vacations planned, holidays executed, home created. This is going to be my time. I reach for my phone to pull up one of Tina's meditation videos because even though my altar has yet to be set up, surely I can consecrate the space with prayer now, right? Realizing I left it on the kitchen counter, I lift the now empty bottle to carry downstairs. I drank an entire bottle of wine? How funny. I haven't done that in years. I've come this far. Why not grab a second? I'll pour a new glass, pull up a meditation video, and chant to the light of the moon. I have all the time in the world and a new space in which to spend it.

Too bad I miscalculated those last steps. Were I not carrying a glass bottle, perhaps I would survive. When I stumble, then fall, my body shatters the glass, piercing the jugular. I don't have time to worry about the mess Mrs. Murdock will have to clean tomorrow. Instead, I follow the light of the moon.

Mother's Little Helper

Lane hums the lyrics of the Rolling Stones tune as she brushes her teeth. It isn't until she's rinsed that she realizes the song is from her dreams. A song she hasn't heard in years. The only Rolling Stones song ever evoked in her daily life is *You Can't Always Get What You Want*, not *Loving Cup*. That is a song from college, but she wasn't dreaming about college, was she?

Lane has time to luxuriate for ten minutes in the shower because it's her husband, Tom's turn with the kids. Long enough to remember her dream from the night before. A dream she knows is recurring, but Lane is ordinarily too busy to concentrate on the specifics. Because she owns an interior design firm and Tom is a busy surgeon, their alternating morning schedule is key to domestic bliss. Tom uses his morning off to stop at the gym and shower there before heading to do rounds at the hospital or see patients at his private practice, conveniently located across the street from each other. Being a cosmetic surgeon has many benefits, including a regular schedule, which is a top priority when raising three small children. There aren't many emergency facelifts or tummy tucks, the type of cosmetic surgeries Tom does. Lane wishes she could say she peacefully writes her gratitudes into a journal with a steaming mug of green tea before practicing yoga, but the reality is Lane uses the time to do a load of laundry, scroll social media, and obsess over the complicated calendar in the kitchen, color labeled for each of their three children. That's only if one of the children doesn't text to ask her to please bring the permission slip, the soccer cleats, and the overdue library book to school on her way to work, requests she receives several times a week.

"You need to let them suffer their consequences, Lane. You're not doing them any favors, running around, making everything perfect for them. Their lives aren't one of your interior design projects," Tom says in exasperation. "Maybe if you didn't rescue them every time, they would be more responsible."

Easy for you to say, buddy, Lane thinks but doesn't speak. Why bother? After twenty years of marriage, Tom isn't going to change who he is. Besides, Tom doesn't understand that compared to other mothers, Lane is far from being a helicopter parent. Tom doesn't know some mothers volunteer at their children's school practically full-time just so they are on the premises with their children. She isn't even on the PTA because they meet during the work week in the middle of the day. Who has that kind of time? Even if Lane weren't a successful designer, she would at least earn money and substitute teach if she felt the need to hover like that.

She cues up Rolling Stones on her drive to school (yes, she is bringing Emily the packed lunch sitting on the center of the kitchen counter. Shut up, Tom) and barks a laugh to *Tumbling Dice*. Lane parks in front of the school and waits for the song to finish before dropping off the lunch. Only after she pulls away from school does she let the tears flow, remembering. She knows what she's been dreaming about, or at least about whom she has been dreaming. Joshua. Always Joshua. No matter she has spent twenty years forgetting him. Her subconscious is knocking. In response, Lane cues up *Can't You Hear Me Knocking*, a song Joshua never performed on stage.

As Lane drives to the furniture warehouse to meet her business partner, Carrie, the memories of practicing lyrics of *Tumbling Dice* over and over with Joshua are too strong to ignore. She and Joshua rented an attic space, apartment too generous a word to describe the one room the slum lord deemed an apartment to charge a stupid amount of rent. Lane and Joshua hid their bed, a mattress on the floor flanked by milk crates on either side, behind a tapestry they hung from the slanted ceiling and delighted over the tiny refrigerator, one-burner range, and tiny porcelain sink that made up the kitchen in the far corner. A futon folded out for the musicians who flopped with them after gigs. Too poor for curtains, Lane filled the windows with potted snake and hanging spider plants. Books lined the walls under the guitars Joshua hung with hooks, their only nod to interior design other than the poster of Frank Zappa that had cost a fortune to frame.

Lane blushes as she remembers the orgasm that her dream evoked. When was the last time that happened? Lane used to have orgasms in her sleep when she was younger, but sex was the furthest thing from her mind these days. Masturbating was almost a chore, something she did quickly, and only because she read somewhere it was healthy for her body. Something about releasing hormones or endorphins, maybe. And Lane is lazy about the task. Lucky to have found the wand, she accomplishes the task with the same efficiency she does brushing her teeth. What used to be an erotic relationship with Tom had trickled into the quiet, ordinary weekly connection couples learn so as not to wake the babies.

The whole thing is ironic, though. In the two years Lane and Joshua lived together, she never had an orgasm during intercourse. As a couple, they were more interested in staying up late to discuss philosophy and existentialism and smoke weed than having sex. They were a meeting of minds, best friends with a shorthand usually reserved for old married couples. For example, if they were watching a movie, Lane could say, "Isn't that the actor from? You know—"

"No, that's the other guy from that show—"

"Oh, right," Lane would respond, both knowing to whom the other was referring without finishing their sentences. There was no need to finish sentences when their minds, souls, and thoughts were connected, if not their bodies. Joshua considered himself asexual if pressed. Something about his fastidious nature inhibited his idea of the messy reality of sex. Almost as if he felt his consciousness to be on a higher realm than to demean it with something as base as sweat, secretions, and sticky sheets. Instead, he preferred to reach ecstasy on stage, insisting the music inspired cosmic orgasms more potent than anything the human body could offer.

Consequently, Lane never opened up to Joshua in bed. He wasn't interested. She was inhibited and unsure of her sexuality, not knowing how to deal with a partner's lack of interest. When they broke up, Lane decided she would seek a partner more interested in sex than which chord to play to segue from song to song on stage. Joshua's abandonment hurt her. She didn't even know if she would trust a man again, but certainly not another musician. What attracted Lane to Tom when they met was his tie, haircut, career, and to be completely honest, because he was Chinese. Lane's mother never visited her apartment when Lane lived with Joshua. She was relieved her daughter's wild phase in college, living with a white boy rock star, was finally over, and Lane's real life as a doctor's wife and mother to her Chinese family could begin.

The first time Lane and Tom had sex, on the verge of orgasm, Lane knew if she were courageous enough to touch her clitoris, she would come. When she did, it drove Tom over the edge, and from there, their sex life skyrocketed until it quietly fizzled these past few years. But that was to be expected when you are parents raising three very active children. Surely, it would rekindle again in the future. Lane isn't worried about that. What concerns her is why her dreams conjure up Joshua after all these years. As she pulls into the warehouse parking lot to meet Carrie, Lane has a sinking feeling this isn't the first dream about Joshua. She knows he has appeared more often than she cares to admit.

"Are you okay?" Carrie asks as they search the warehouse for the pieces they need to stage the house. These clients are particularly demanding, and the job has lingered almost a week longer than Lane anticipated.

"I just haven't been sleeping well lately," Lane says as she triumphantly holds the lamp aloft. "Yes! This is it. Now we just need that damn table. Look over there, please."

The rest of the day is a blur once the women locate the pieces and drive to the client's home to finish the project. Lane operates on autopilot as she retrieves the children from school, dropping one at ballet and the other at soccer practice, then hustles to prepare dinner as the children arrive home minutes before Tom. Family dinner, dishes, homework, and two loads of laundry because Lane's daughter absolutely had to have her favorite pink shirt tomorrow, regardless her mother was loading the dryer. Lane merely sighs, accepts the shirt, and runs a second load. There's always more laundry to do in the house.

Lane is so exhausted, irrationally irritated with the click of chopsticks against bowls when her family eats dinner. Of course, like most American families, they usually eat with forks and knives, but practicing chopsticks is something Lane and Tom force their children to do every year the few weeks before Chinese New Year to stave off the glaring criticism they will receive from their mothers if the children can't use chopsticks. It's bad enough the children can only say a few basic phrases in Chinese. Her irritability intensifies as the evening wanes. Lane clenches her teeth when Tom clips his toenails at the side of the bed. It doesn't matter that he carefully collects them into a tissue to dispose. She has asked him a million times to do that in the bathroom, yet he never listens. Finally, Lane suffers a flash of irrational anger when she hears her husband snoring. How he can fall asleep the moment his head hits the pillow is beyond her. It takes Lane at least an hour to silence the endless lists that run through her mind. Lane glances at her emails, removes Tom's glasses, places them on the bedside table, clicks off the television, and goes to sleep.

Who is blasting music this early on a school day, Lane wonders when she awakens the next morning. Is that *Wild Horses*? Her children only listen to Disney-safe hip-hop and pop music, not the Rolling Stones. Lane rolls over for Tom, but the bed is empty. She abruptly sits up and gasps.

She is back in her attic apartment, behind the tapestry. How can this be? Dreams have never been this vivid, certainly not enough to include music she clearly hears, but when the tea kettle whistles, she is shocked to her core. Lane and Tom drink coffee, not tea. In fact, Lane hasn't drunk tea since her days with Joshua, not even at New Year's Dinner, much to her mother's chagrin.

Lane pushes back the tapestry to find Joshua preparing tea in the mugs they made together at a ceramics class before Joshua dropped out to pursue music with his band. Lane wonders where those mugs went. She hasn't seen them in twenty years.

"Good morning," Joshua says, handing her the tea and kissing her on the cheek. "I'm sorry the music woke you, but I need it to inspire this new song. You know how I am when I'm writing. I've been up all night. Do you want to hear it? Let me turn this down so I can play it for you, okay?"

Lane forgot how much Joshua talked. His rapid-fire monologue is jarring after spending the past twenty years with her quiet husband. Lane sits on the futon as Joshua clicks off the Rolling Stones, picks up his guitar, and squints over the lyrics he's scribbled on a yellow legal pad. She immediately recognizes the song and takes that as evidence this is absolutely a dream—a realistic, incredibly vivid dream, but a dream, nonetheless. The song is the one that garners the attention of a major record label and goes on to launch Joshua's band into the national spotlight.

"Into the light she goes," Lane interrupts Joshua.

He picks up his head, startled.

Lane says, "The lyric should read, *into the light she goes.*"

Joshua nods, leans over his legal pad, and makes scratches on the page. "Yes. That makes sense. That sounds better."

He picks up his guitar and continues. Lane nods along and begins to sing. Joshua stops and asks, "I haven't gotten further than that. What do you think, Yoko?"

Lane tries not to grimace at the nickname. Joshua knows how much it irritates her when the band teases them by calling them John and Yoko. Yoko is Japanese, not Chinese. It's infuriating when people think all Asian people are the same, from the same country, same culture. Furthermore, Yoko is credited with breaking up The Beatles, and Lane resents the implication that she would do the same. Especially now that she's forty-two years old and knows her younger self didn't break up the band. Just the opposite. She sacrificed her heart for their success.

Feeling disoriented, Lane rises and walks to the bathroom. The reflection of herself in the mirror startles her. She reaches to touch her hair. It's long again. And her face. Lane doesn't realize how wrinkled she is becoming until she sees herself. This is weird. And a very long dream. Has Lane ever peed in her dream? Does that mean she is peeing the bed, at home, next to Tom?

Lane gasps and sits up. Tom turns over and mumbles, "Ten more minutes."

Lane reaches for her phone, which reads five-fifty in the morning, precisely ten minutes before Tom rises like clockwork. She touches her hair, cut blunt at her jawline, and without looking, knows it is streaked with gray, not the long, almost blue-black her hair was when she was twenty. Because it's her turn with the children, Lane doesn't ponder the dream even as it hovers in her peripheral vision as she assembles lunches and cuts fruit to be eaten with breakfast cereal before shuttling the children to the bus stop, but she does try to confide in Carrie as they eat lunch together.

"I had no idea you were a groupie," Carrie says, eyes widening. "You lived with a musician before you met Tom? When was this, in college?"

"First of all, I wasn't a groupie. I was the lead singer's girlfriend. There's a big difference. I wasn't one of those girls who hung out at the stage door. I knew Joshua before he was Joshua Brenner," Lane says without thinking.

Carrie almost chokes on her sandwich and says, "You were Joshua Brenner's lover? Are you serious? How have you never told me that?"

"Because it was twenty years ago, something I don't discuss with Tom, and a time in my life I'd prefer to forget," Lane says. "That's why I'm so confused. I'm not talking about just one dream. I've had several, and last night's? Let's just say it was so vivid, I'm still not quite sure it didn't happen. I know that sounds crazy. Of course, it didn't happen, but Carrie. It was just so real."

"Listen, you're exhausted. We've been working our asses off to finish this house, and it's taking a toll on you, that's all. What you need is a long rest. Maybe you and Tom should book a weekend away together. We'll be done with the house by Friday, and our next project doesn't start for what? Two weeks? You have time. Take it," Carrie says.

"You're right," Lane says because it's easier to agree than explain how complicated her family weekend plans are to her friend, who is childless and single by choice. Practices, games, and rehearsals are scheduled months in advance. If Lane and Tom wanted to go away together, it would take almost military precision in tactical scheduling of that complicated color-coded calendar in the kitchen, a thought that exhausts Lane as she studies it that evening while the children feast on pizzas delivered. Lane opts for the easiest route in her disoriented state, a special treat for everyone, not requiring chopsticks and patience. She is careful with her tone in guiding the children through homework, bath, and bed and solicitous to Tom, bringing him a bowl of vanilla ice cream with a slice of cantaloupe, his favorite. At bedtime, Lane lingers in the hallway, studying the picture gallery instead of her ordinary thoughtlessness, taking for granted the family she built and the memories they created.

"I'm going to take a bath," Lane says to Tom, who is already in bed, watching television. She fills the tub with lavender-infused Epsom salts and adds a dollop of bubbles. As it fills, she washes her face and moisturizes, realizing the money she has spent for twenty years hasn't really done much compared to the face she remembers from last night's dream. No amount of Botox or plastic surgery can recreate dewy youthfulness, so beyond moisturizing and the occasional facial, Lane has accepted reality. She thanks her Chinese genes, knowing she looks at least ten years younger than Carrie, who is the same age. So, at least there's that, even though Lane winces at how petty that sentiment is.

Feeling relaxed, Lane surprises Tom by initiating sex, which is good, satisfying for them both in their quiet, accustomed manner. Tom mumbles, "Love you," as he drifts to sleep.

In the morning, Lane isn't surprised to wake in the attic. Again, she finds Joshua in the living room, yellow legal pad on the table, guitar on his lap.

"I've written more. Want to hear?"

Lane nods and perches on the other end of the futon. She remembers these pajama bottoms, the owl print once her favorite, which she wears with a white tank top. Big mistake. She should not have looked down. Lane doesn't believe her breasts, perky before nursing three children, and resists the urge to cup them to feel their buoyancy.

Instead, Lane focuses on how beautiful twenty-two-year-old Joshua looks in the morning light, brow furrowed over his guitar, singing softly.

Before the fame, before the Grammys, before the record-breaking, sold-out shows, Joshua is the poet Lane loves, and she has forgotten how much she misses him. She could sit forever in this private moment, listening to him sing softly, just to her, but he gets the lyrics wrong.

"Wait," Lane says. "It goes like this." She sings the song she has known for twenty years, the song that still plays on the radio, the song that won Joshua his first number-one single. She sings it, replete with the hums, little snatches of repeated words, everything exactly how it will be recorded before she can stop herself.

In the silence, Joshua is open-mouthed before he picks up his pen and begins frantically scribbling as Lane's heart pounds. What has she done? She didn't write the song when they lived together in college, did she? She wracks her brain, trying to remember Joshua writing the song, but the memories are hazy, and because when wasn't Joshua writing, singing, strumming? Music was breathing to Joshua. From the moment he woke until he fell asleep, songs came to him in his dreams. Driving down the road, in the shower, he scrawled on endless post-it notes. Joshua hummed even when running errands, picking apples at the market, replacing a lightbulb.

"What was the chord switch again?" Joshua asks. "Before the chorus? Can you sing that part again?"

Lane obliges. She quietly sings the entire song from beginning to end as Joshua nods and takes notes. When she finishes, he says, "How have I never known how beautifully you sing? Did you write this yourself? When did you write it?"

"It's not my song," Lane says, leaning over to kiss his cheek. She inhales deeply, remembering the combination of sandalwood, tobacco, and the very essence that is Joshua.

"It's yours."

Before he can reply, Lane hears, "Mommy?" and turns. She opens her eyes to find her youngest standing at her bedside. "I had a nightmare. May I tuck in, please?"

Lane lifts the sheet in answer and spoons her baby while brushing the silky bangs from her forehead, whispering Joshua's song to lull her child to sleep.

Stardust

Irene tugs the bodice of the blue silk dress her husband chose as an anniversary gift for her to wear. She loves and resents the idea that she has remained the same dress size for forty years, probably able to squeeze into her wedding dress if she were inclined, but who has time for nostalgia after raising eight children? She keeps her figure only because she never sits down, not because she tortures herself with a fitness routine although she eats like a bird. Maybe that's the wrong analogy, Irene wonders. Didn't she read that birds consume twice their weight? When the children were home, Irene existed on Mother's rations, scraps of food the children didn't eat. A nibble of scrambled egg from Denise's plate, a crust of toast from Laura's, and the last of Tony's orange juice was more than enough breakfast for a five-foot woman. She skips lunch but eats dinner at the table every single night at six o'clock, except on Sundays when they eat a mid-day meal after Mass.

Irene's children never ate a morsel before communion. Only after they returned from Mass could the children nibble on antipasto, as the vat of gravy she set at dawn simmers, before the family feasted with chicken parmesan or lasagna, huge beef meatballs, and wilted greens. They gathered for Sunday dinner in the dining room where Irene taught her children proper manners at a perfectly set table with a lace tablecloth, the good china, and silver. Irene still rolls and cuts pasta the day before, continuing the heritage both Irene and her husband, Frank learned from their own Italian Catholic families. Routine and tradition, like the custom of gifting her a dress Frank chooses, enjoying the process of walking into Shillito's Department Store and consulting with Margaret, the same salesperson who helps him purchase the dress she kindly wraps in tissue paper and their signature cream satin ribbon before sliding it into a handled shopping bag, thus saving Frank the extra step of having to wrap a gift. Irene accepts the bag, slips into the dress, and they spend the evening dancing at Moonlite Gardens to whatever big band plays tunes by Glenn Miller, Count Basie, Duke Ellington, and of course, a Frank Sinatra tune or two.

Irene gazes at the entrance, looking past the arches to the balcony elegantly flanked with scrolled balustrade. The white building elicits romance with its Romanesque style and mosaic marble dance floor where Irene and Frank have spent forty anniversary evenings in each other's arms. Where is he? Surely, Frank will materialize momentarily, and they will laugh when he explains he got caught up talking with one of his clients because selling insurance is what Frank does to support their family. Maintaining a reputation as a well-mannered family man is key to Frank's success, Irene reminds herself, pulling her shoulders back and lifting her chin.

Irene can hear the familiar strains of *Moonlight Serenade* and fights her impatience. She lifts her hand to wave to a man she spies on the balcony. Because he is wearing Frank's hat, Irene assumes it is her husband, looking for her, so she walks away from the fountain in front of the venue and enters the building. She climbs the stairs to the balcony, where she saw Frank from below, but she doesn't find him as she walks the length, so Irene stops in the center, grips the railing, and looks down. Couples are beginning to fill the dance floor. Not yet dusk, the band is lively with anticipation. Scanning the periphery, Irene doesn't spot Frank's signature hat. She watches the fading sun reflect off the Ohio River behind the building. Irene's attention is interrupted when she smells pipe tobacco, the same scent of the tobacco her father favored. She turns to see a stranger.

"Hey there, girlie. Where's your feller?" the man asks Irene.

"I'm not sure," Irene says. She worries the old man is holding his hand out to invite her to dance until she looks into his palm and sees a tarnished coin. When she frowns at him, he says, "Obolus. Here. Take. I'm done with mine."

The coin feels cold in her hand, making her shiver in the night air. She turns to thank the old man, but he disappeared. The wail of the clarinet commands her attention back to the band playing a song, accelerating the tempo as the dancers keep time. Feeling dizzy from watching the women spin around and around, Irene stumbles back down the stairs and out of Moonlite Gardens.

Irene stands in line at a dock, waiting to board a riverboat ferry. She can hear ragtime music, people on board laughing, champagne corks popping as she studies the four-storied white steamboat detailed in red, matching its large red paddlewheel, contrasting the large black stacks. It's past dusk, and Irene is worried, still looking for Frank. Perhaps this is an anniversary surprise. The que moves slowly, giving Irene time to study the water that reflects the moon and stars on the water, confusing her senses. Where is she? She looks for evidence this is the Ohio River and where she is supposed to be. When she reaches the front of the line, a man in a red bowtie and red suspenders over a white striped shirt and black pants wears a nametag that reads, *Caron*. The man says, "Obolus, ma'am?"

"I'm waiting for my husband," Irene says, attempting to step aside.

"Only room for one on this passage," he says. Holding his hand upturned, he repeats, "Obolus."

Irene stumbles backward, away from the line, confused. She is about to hand him the obolus when she hears Frank speak her name. Relieved, she turns away from the man in the red bowtie and says, "I'm not boarding. You may go. I'm going to stay behind."

Irene hears the man in the red bowtie call, "Are you sure, miss? You're ready to cross. Just give me the obolus, and we can launch. It's that easy. We're waiting for you."

About to Run

"Damn, it's hot. How can it be this hot in October?" Toni grumbles as she and her wife, Willow, exit the Phoenix, Arizona airport, pulling their luggage to wait for their driver to whisk them away to the Waldorf Astoria, where Toni is counting on a Bloody Mary to soothe her nerves. Only one layover in Atlanta to fly from Ohio to Arizona without any glitches, yet Toni is a nervous traveler. And she has no interest in the two shows at the Orpheum Theater other than seeing Jennifer Hartswick on stage, the lure Willow dangled to hook Toni, and it worked.

"We've never been to the desert, honey. It's on my bucket list. Don't you want to see the mountains? And listen to this. You love Frank Lloyd Wright. He has something like two hundred houses there. Maybe we can go on a tour to see them," Willow said, looking over her laptop one evening in August when the show tickets were announced. "And it's not Phish. It's Trey Anastasio Band. Big difference. Horns section. Women singers. We'll stay at a posh resort where there aren't any hippies and lounge at the pool. I promise. You'll love it."

Toni was exhausted from a long day packed with one desperate client after the other. Being a therapist was both inspiring and draining, and she had yet to unpack the groceries, begin dinner, and feed the dogs when her wife overwhelmed her with this plan to fly across the country to see two shows, but when she saw that familiar glimmer in Willow's eyes, there was little choice but to agree. Anything to keep Willow happy. And then Toni grimaced, remembering the one client she privately despised who, just today, said in session, "Happy wife/happy life," causing Toni to bend her head down, pretending to take notes so she could arrange the contempt in her face to counsel the idiot. But when Willow wrapped her arms around Toni and placed her head between Toni's shoulder blades, it worked the magic it always does. Consequently, Toni willingly abandoned the autumnal glory that is Ohio in October for the blazing sun in the desert. All for love.

"You're lucky to have come when you did," the driver says. "The heat just broke. It's beautiful now."

"It's ninety-eight degrees," Toni says.

"Right. Perfect, yes?"

Toni pulls her sunglasses from the top of her head and shields her eyes, looking out the window instead of answering the delusional man. How he thinks this is cool weather is obviously evidence he has never been a perimenopausal woman. Whatever. She remains silent, letting Willow do the small talk for which Toni has no patience.

When they arrive at the resort, the grip of anxiety, impatience, and irritation melt away. It is as beautiful as promised from the website, and the research Toni did to learn the ambiguous history of whether Frank Lloyd Wright built the resort or contributed to the design, or it was all built as a tribute to the man. Fascinating. Toni spends hours following research wormholes for fun, something Willow knows about her all too well, using that to entice her to the desert. It wasn't necessary. Toni has followed Willow wherever she goes for over twenty years. From the moment Toni saw the beautiful hippie selling her textile creations at the art fair at Coney Island, she was mesmerized. Some call them an opposite couple, but Toni likes to think they are a complementary couple and is secretly glad she and her wife don't seem to match, mirroring each other like so many lesbian couples they know. How boring to be with someone exactly like yourself. When Willow is in an emotionally and psychologically good place, she says, "I bring fun to your life and a deeper sense of spirituality, and in return, you provide the foundation and security I need as an artist to thrive." When Willow goes dark and twisty into the depths of despair, she laments, "You have all the power in our marriage. I have nothing. Compared to you, I'm a failure. You're better at everything. You earn way more money than I will ever see. You're morally stronger, and you always do the right thing. I don't even know why you stay with me."

No matter how often Toni reassures Willow that she married her for who she is and not for what she does, the same fight cycles, and it even gained intensity during quarantine from the global pandemic. Now that Toni can return to her office every day, she hopes their marriage will steady. Too much time together wreaked havoc on many marriages. Toni knows. At least six of her clients are going through a divorce, which Toni is desperate to avoid in her marriage. If her sweet wife wants to fly to a desert to see her favorite band, Toni books the flights and reserves a suite at the resort that proves to be beyond Toni's expectations. Its balcony overlooks a garden created in rectangles lined in red clay pathways, filled with white pansies and green manicured bushes proudly displaying the Sprite statues, mesmerizing to Toni. She cannot believe the view of the purple mountain to the east, where the sun will rise beyond it tomorrow. She can easily imagine models from Ralph Lauren ads walking their dogs across the green lawns below, exactly how the resort images appeared on the internet.

Once she and her wife change into swimsuits, they walk to one of the restaurants in the resort for lunch and that necessary Bloody Mary.

"Isn't this nice to have the afternoon together and tomorrow before the shows?" Willow asks after they place their orders. It may be three o'clock in the afternoon in Ohio, but it is only noon in Arizona, which feels like a bonus of sorts to Toni. Like stolen time.

"We can go for a hike tomorrow morning if you like. Or schedule the history tour of the resort," Willow continues. "Or lounge at the pool or sleep in. Whatever you want, honey."

Toni smiles. Whenever Willow knows Toni is indulging her, Willow goes into overdrive to please Toni in return. Twenty years ago, it was a dynamic Toni tried to break. Now, she accepts her wife's contrition because Willow is like a whirling dervish when she is in the middle of a weaving project, despondent when she is rejected from being included in a festival or show, or worse, accepted but doesn't sell a single piece. Toni reminds herself how boring her life would be without Willow, even though her mercurial nature can be exhausting. Artists need more reassurance than other people, in Toni's experience, so she digs deeply to find grace and forgiveness because ordinary people don't depend their income on what Willow calls her heart and soul, her art. Toni acknowledges the risk of vulnerability it takes to be an artist, and what's more? She admires her wife's talent, so devoting her life to supporting and encouraging an artist feels satisfying to Toni.

Toni ignores Willow's excitement about the enormous waterslide at the family pool and bypasses it without comment to the adult pool, which reveals itself to be a paradise, barely populated on this quiet Sunday afternoon. Under an umbrella, they settle on chaise lounges. Toni hands Willow her digital reader and sunblock and unearths a copy of *The Lincoln Highway*.

"I can't believe you'd rather lug around a book the size of *War and Peace* instead of a skinny little reader," Willow says.

When Toni doesn't respond, Willow abandons her reader for the pool. As she floats on one of the many inflatables available, something Toni has never seen at a resort and is impressed by, she turns her attention back to Amor Towles' brilliant book. An avid reader, there are only two other authors whose writing is so stunning it causes Toni to stop reading to marvel at the craft. Toni Morrison and Margaret Atwood. And now this Amor guy. The story is so engrossing; Toni barely noticed the four-hour flight, and she is delighted the book will probably last until their return flight because, after two hours at the pool, Toni entices Willow back to the room to make love. Reading can wait.

The following day after a five-mile run along the canal and breakfast of egg whites and fruit, Toni and Willow return to the pool, first stopping to marvel at The Wise One named Lloyd, a seven-thousand-pound, thirty-three-foot cactus planted in 1882. Toni is disappointed the promised historical tour of the resort is only offered on the weekends, but Willow is so excited for the show, her exuberance compensates for this minor glitch in planning, especially when, in their room, dressing for dinner and the show, Willow offers a gift she hid in their suitcase.

"These are the shoes Jennifer Hartswick wore on stage for the Beacon shows," Willow says, holding up the white sequined sneakers. Toni is delighted. The shoes match perfectly with her T-shirt that reads, "Girl, Woman, Goddess, Shit" in blue glitter letters, which she dons with wide yoga pants that split down the middle of each leg, like air conditioning a menopausal woman appreciates when it's ninety degrees in Arizona.

Because the women have never been to Phoenix, they choose to dine at the resort's Mexican restaurant, an excellent and efficient choice. They order smoked Wagyu beef brisket with roasted peppers Toni pairs with a lovely Malbec as the waiter offers tortilla chips, guacamole, and three different salsas to start. Toni smiles when Willow excuses herself to use the restroom because, dressed in a silk patchwork open-back dress exposing sun-kissed skin, Willow turns every head in the restaurant. To kill time, Toni scrolls social media, a decision she will regret. Maybe Willow is right. If Toni had *The Lincoln Highway* on a slim digital reader, she would not have opened her phone. As soon as they return to Ohio, Toni will purchase one.

"What is it?" Willow says when she returns to the table. One glance, and she knows. Toni hesitates. Willow has been ebullient all day in anticipation of the shows. It's not just the sun that makes her wife glow.

And they have second-row seats tonight. How can Toni share what she saw with Willow? How can she not? Stalling, Toni sips her wine.

"Honey, I'm not sure I should tell you this because it's bad news. But how can I not tell you? You already sense something," Toni says. "I mean, even if I chose not to tell you, you would know something was wrong. I'm going to buy a digital reader."

"What?" Willow says, confused. "A digital reader is bad news? Damn. You scared the shit out of me."

Willow dips a chip into the guacamole and smiles as she chews. Just as Toni opens her mouth to correct her wife, the waiter arrives with the entrée with the flourish a Wagyu brisket that has been smoked for twelve hours deserves. Toni waits patiently as the waiter explains the intensity of each pepper's heat and which sauce to pair as they heap slices of the succulent meat onto soft blue tortillas. Toni can't taste the first bite, which rests like sawdust on her tongue, her grief so thick.

"Honey, Melinda died," Toni says. "Olivia posted it just now, and I saw it, and I don't know whether I should have told you, but how can I not tell you? I'm so sorry."

Willow tilts her head like she does when she is confused, but when she meets Toni's eyes, her eyes fill with tears. Willow reaches into her handbag and retrieves her phone. "It's on Olivia's wall? You know I don't follow her."

Toni pushes her plate aside and finishes her wine as Willow scrolls.

"Did you see this?" Willow says, offering the phone to Toni, who accepts it to study the image Melinda posted as a banner on her page. It is a haunting sepia-toned image of ghosts hanging from trees and a realistic silhouette of a witch flying on a broom.

Before Toni can say what they both know, Willow grabs the phone back and says, "I'm going to text Olivia."

Toni signals for the waiter to box their food and to request their check, explaining they just received news a friend died. Not only did the staff swiftly respond, a confection of meringue caramel dessert arrives, "A small sweet to offer our condolences."

When the women return to their room to refrigerate the dinner they didn't eat, Toni asks, "Do you still want to go to the show? What did Olivia say, honey?"

"She thanked me for reaching out and said Melinda went in to take a nap and never woke up. That she had suffered from Graves' disease and bipolar depression and that she died in her sleep. I think I'm in shock. I know I'm in shock. I'm stunned."

Toni sits next to her wife on the edge of the bed and puts her arm around her because there is nothing else to do. Of course, Willow is in shock. One of the reasons Toni agreed to this vacation was to celebrate the seventh anniversary, what Willow calls her Rebirthday, from when Willow purposefully overdosed to commit suicide, only to be rescued by Toni. Willow suffered a harrowing week in the hospital and then devoted seven years in therapy to recover, a milestone Toni respects. She worries how Willow will respond to this blow today, of all days, two days before Willow's Rebirthday, when her wife suddenly stands up and snaps, "Of course we're still going to the show. Melinda would want us to go to the show. You know how many Grateful Dead shows she and I saw together. We did not come all the way out here to not go to the shows. This is fucking ridiculous. I'm devastated. Of course I am. But I'm alive, goddammit. I'm alive. Let's go."

Knowing better than to argue with her wife when she gets into these moods, Toni simply nods and follows.

Their driver says, "You know the Orpheum Theater is haunted, yes?"

"Of course it is. We know all about ghosts," Willow says, then turns to Toni, offering a mushroom, saying, "Want to eat just a little bit with me?"

"Are you sure, Willow?" Toni says, accepting the cap as she watches her wife gulp water to wash down the handful she swallows. It's too late to say, *maybe not so much.*

Once they find their seats, Willow asks Toni to take pictures of her in front of the gold-painted columns of the theater. Their second-row seats are on the aisle next to the wall of the theater, which is wonderful because Willow is a wild dancer who likes a lot of room, and nobody will pass by them like they would, seated in the center aisle. Meanwhile, Toni is content to sit in a seat like she likes, especially as the first wave of dreaminess the mushrooms evoke as the trip begins.

The crowd roars as the band take the stage and launch the show with a quick *Mozambique,* energizing dancing before segueing into *Everything's Right.* Toni watches Willow as she dances with her arms over her head, stomping her feet, singing along with gusto through *Alive Again.* Toni wipes away a tear, grateful her wife is joyously alive again, until the band plays *Ghost, Sweet Dreams Melinda,* and *Olivia.* How the fuck can this be? Is Toni hallucinating this far? She follows as Willow breaks away during

Olivia, exits the theater, and walks downstairs to the women's room, one of those old-fashioned restrooms found in country clubs, featuring a parlor with velvet settees and chairs separate from the space of mirrors and sinks, separate from the lavatories.

Toni spies a woman offering candy to console Willow, who is crying in front of the sinks. "No, thank you," Willow says. "I don't need candy. My friend died. I'm just sad. But thank you."

Toni smiles reassuringly at the woman before she asks her wife, "Are you okay, honey?" She directs Willow to sit with her on the velvet settee.

"These mushrooms are really powerful," Willow says. "I keep feeling like there's someone over my right shoulder. It's weird. I keep turning around, but there's no one there. Do you think it's the ghost or the mushrooms? You don't think it's Melinda, do you? And how can the band have known to play these songs? I'm freaking out a little bit."

"Okay, but they also played *Alive Again*. That means something, too," Toni says. "Take a deep breath, and let's practice our mantra, shall we? Seven years. The human body sheds skin cells which means—"

Willow picks up, "Every seven years, we have a whole new body of skin, and this skin, this skin on my body that swam in a pool under an Arizona sky today, is new. This skin didn't die. This skin is alive. I'm alive."

"That's right. How do you feel?" Toni says, looking into Willow's eyes, whose pupils are dilated from the psychedelics. When Willow breaks into a smile, she jumps up, offers her hand to her wife, and says, "Better. Let's go. I don't want to miss the end of first set."

The couple weaves their way back to their space just as the band plays the first notes of *Set Your Soul Free*. Toni chooses to dance in the aisle with her wife instead of taking her seat in the row; she's so relieved, even though she's still worried. They are only halfway through the show.

Second set soothes Toni with one of her favorite songs, *Drifting*, and she is delighted to hear *Curlew's Call*. This older song floats her back to their early days of marriage, cooking spaghetti in the kitchen, drinking red wine out of Mason jars, and dancing barefoot. Toni's revelry is jolted when Trey wails, *About to Run*. She watches Willow dance, tears streaming down her face. *Sand* is redemption, but to end the encore with *Life Beyond a Dream* is healing. Toni wraps her arms around Willow's waist as they sway and sing along with the band, and everyone connects in the audience under this magical spell.

As soon as the band takes their final bows, Willow grabs Toni's hand and makes a beeline outside, saying, "Call for a car now, please," bypassing the hiss of nitrous tanks, groups of folks lighting cigarettes, and the general post-show merriment. Fortunately, a car arrives within minutes, driving them to the resort in silence. Instead of her usual banter, Willow stares out the window as Toni holds her hand and thanks the driver.

Once they enter their room, Willow takes a shower while Toni pours herself a glass of wine. Although she only microdosed, she needs help coming down from the energy psychedelics provide. Changing into a caftan, she opens her phone, slipping on her reading glasses to look at the day's pictures while sipping wine. She stops scrolling and zooms in to get a closer look at the picture she took of Willow in front of the gold-painted columns. Cast in a vivid purple light, a shadow of what looks like a woman with bent arms, mimicking angel wings, floats on top of Willow as if superimposed. The shadow is not behind Willow, and the shadow is not a reflection of Toni, whose hair was pulled into a bun for the show. The shadow's hair is to her shoulders, shorter than Willow's. What exactly is she seeing?

"This is going to sound weird," Willow says, exiting the bathroom in a robe, her hair wound in a towel turban. "But I think Melinda's ghost entered me."

"What do you mean, entered you?" Toni asks, turning her phone face down and placing it on the bedside table.

"You know how I said I kept thinking there was somebody behind me? I kept feeling a presence over my right shoulder," Willow says. "I couldn't shake it. Even after we chanted the mantra in the restroom, I still felt it, so when Trey sang *About to Run*, I lifted my arms and said, 'Okay, Melinda. I will let you enter me for this one show. You may dance through me tonight, but only tonight. I will share this with you. But Melinda. You are dead, and I'm alive, and I plan to stay that way.' Suddenly, I felt free. I don't know how to explain it, but I honestly feel like she entered me, and offering her that gift reinforces my goal to stay alive. Toni, I want to live. I want to live."

Willow puts her face into her hands and begins to sob. Toni stands, pours a glass of water, retrieves a box of tissues, and returns to the bed. "Would you also like some wine?"

"No wine, thank you. I'm sorry. I know I've said it before, but you have no idea the guilt I carry. I'm sorry, Toni," Willow says, accepting the water and wiping her tears with a tissue. "I hate that I put you through that nightmare. I love you."

"Willow, I love you, honey. I forgive you. I'm just glad you're alive. I need you, my dear one. You are the love of my life. The dream of my dreams. My end-all, be-all. Now try to get some sleep. We can talk about this tomorrow."

Toni watches as her wife drifts to sleep. She doesn't need to examine the picture again. Her wife told her everything she needs to know, and maybe Willow doesn't need to know what she saw, and sometimes that is love.

Backward Down the Number Line

Lucy stands at the sink, faucet running while she stares at the rain through the kitchen window. She worries it won't subside by tomorrow when the party preparations begin in earnest. It's too silent, she thinks as she stacks the last of the dishes on the rack to dry, so she cues up The Carpenters to play *Rainy Days and Mondays* on the kitchen speaker even though it's Wednesday. Lucy has always loved this song but can't stand the rest of the siblings' catalog and especially cringes when she sees images of cadaverous Karen, so Lucy switches to Coltrane after singing the last bars about Mondays. Rain calls for *In a Sentimental Mood* and all things jazz, as far as Lucy is concerned, and she wants to spare herself from her husband, Doug's teasing about her nostalgic attachment to folk music. Of course, she never played sappy songs when her children were in high school and still lived at home. They tolerated Grateful Dead because they had no choice. It is practically a prerequisite to living in Woodstock, New York. But like all kids, they had their own ideas about their tastes in music.

Lucy cracks two eggs and separates the yolks, discarding the whites before cracking a third egg and whisking it to a foam. She fills a pot with water to boil linguine before dicing onions and garlic to sauté in olive oil in a skillet. The red pepper she roasted earlier, its black skin shed, seeds and stems removed, lay on a wood cutting board to be sliced to add to the carbonara. A small dish of verdant green peas Lucy purchased at the farmer's market lay ready. Oregano, never basil, cracked black pepper, freshly grated parmesan cheese, and so much salt it makes the water taste like the ocean are the last ingredients to make Lucy's famous carbonara for dinner. Instead of pancetta, Lucy likes to use thick-cut hardwood bacon she bakes on a stone pan until it crumbles at the touch, a trick she adopted when her daughter had her wisdom teeth removed and couldn't eat the too-gummy pancetta but was pleading for her favorite dinner.

"I picked up the garlic loaf you requested," Doug says as he unleashes Charlie Brown, who shakes his coat, wet from the rain.

"I got it. I got it," Doug says before Lucy can protest, as he reaches into the drawer for a towel, using it to dry his head before the dog's fur.

"I'm glad it's raining. The gardens need the water," Doug says. "And excellent timing, too. Forecast predicting clear skies and sunshine all weekend, I promise."

How can you promise when you're a musician, not a weather forecaster? Lucy bites back the bitchiness. She knows the nerves, not Doug, have her on edge. Hence, the comfort of a bowl of pasta on an ordinary rainy Wednesday in June. That and a hefty glass of wine will cheer the maudlin mood that descended on Lucy the longer the afternoon stretched.

She hands her husband a glass of wine and says, "Twenty minutes until dinner." Doug kisses her cheek and retreats to the living room to switch on the television. She is embarrassed to admit after their children left home, she and Doug rarely sit at the dining room table to eat, instead choosing to watch shows like other boring middle-aged couples, replete with the volume turned up loud like the geriatric hearing aid commercials, no matter that their hearing loss is due to rock and roll shows. No street cred when you're fifty, and inevitable age creeps in. It is what it is, and Lucy learned to accept that through menopause, while Doug still thinks he can lift any weight and stay up as late as he likes, illusions Lucy doesn't bother to shatter even as she pulls a blanket over him when he falls asleep on the sofa most evenings before ten when not working a late session in one of the various studios in the city where he plays keyboards and piano.

There will be no early evenings this weekend, Lucy can easily predict. Not when friends reunite after twenty-five years. Not merely friends but housemates and even more intimately involved as former bandmates. Doug planned the party for Saturday evening, so everyone will arrive at various times Friday, and apparently, no one plans to depart until Monday. Lucy bends over her phone to jot yet another note, this reminder to stop for fresh flowers for each guest house on their property. Woodstock Field to Vase will provide elaborate flower designs for Saturday's party, but Lucy wants to arrange small bouquets for each of their friends herself. Little personal touches and attention to detail are important to Lucy and help distract her from the idea that she and Amelia will see each other for the first time in all these years.

Lucy is startled when Gloria Gaynor's song, *Never Can Say Goodbye*, blasts from the speakers. How did this song end up on her jazz playlist? As her shoulders almost instinctually sway to the bop, Lucy is transported to junior high on Saturday mornings, glued to Amelia's television, watching 1970s reruns of *Soul Train*. Lucy and Amelia at twelve, then thirteen, and fourteen, danced in front of the screen until Amelia's mother shooed them away from the only television in the house. Memories stack like panes of glass, reminding Lucy of Jean-Pierre Weill's paintings on multiple layers of glass. Less memory of a single moment than stacking of six years their families lived next door to each other on Sherwood Forest Lane, then four years as college roommates, first in the dorms, and finally in the house with everyone else in the band. Lucy and Amelia at fifteen, sixteen, seventeen at school dances, prom, nightclubs. Nineteen, twenty, twenty-two, dancing at Grateful Dead and Phish shows. By twenty-three, Lucy danced on the wings as Amelia danced on stage, microphone in hand as lead singer.

Amelia was naturally gifted with rhythm that matched her incredible vocal ability, skills she now uses in front of packed auditoriums on stage as one of the world's most famous contemporary neo-soul artists. Twelve-year-old Lucy tried to follow her best friend's steps, extending the *Soul Train* line onto the shag carpet of Amelia's family room, but she was never a very good dancer and certainly couldn't carry a tune. Instead, Lucy's voice sings on the page. First, in a diary, pouring out her heart and soul; then as an English major in college, attempting to write shitty poems; and now as a professional writer, stuck writing a series her contract won't allow her to escape. She was never jealous of Amelia's singing and dancing abilities. She was jealous of Amelia's hair beautifully braided in thick rows ending in shells and beads.

Comparatively, Amelia's lank mousy hair fell flat, both literally and figuratively. What Amelia never knew, what Lucy would be too embarrassed to admit to anyone, were the private moments, alone in her bedroom, in front of the mirror. Twelve-year-old Lucy would wrap a towel around her head like a turban to mimic the beautiful Black queen, "Beautiful people use Afro Sheen." In Lucy's imagination, her cotton nightgown transformed into a Kente cloth caftan. In her hand, a hairbrush served as microphone as Lucy hit play on the cassette, practicing lyrics as backup singer, never star. Lucy never wanted to be in the spotlight. She fantasized about the beauty of an afro. She romanticized Amelia, considering her exotic in comparison to Lucy's crowded Italian Catholic family in a Youngstown, Ohio neighborhood where everyone knew everyone. When the Washington family moved next door, it was the most exciting thing to happen to Lucy. A born star, Amelia flourished under Lucy's gaze.

A month before sixth grade was sufficient time to become fast friends to face junior high school together. They rode a new yellow bus that picked them up at the corner of their street with older kids, Marnie Nichols, Patty Sullivan, and brothers Joseph and Jacob Brady. Lucy initiated a routine on the first day of school when she rang Amelia's doorbell to walk to the bus stop together. Sixth grade in a new building, riding on a bus with older kids was intimidating, awkward, and horribly smelly, if Lucy remembers correctly.

Of course, she remembers the smells, if from nothing else than the experience of her two junior-high children's body odors, her son a bit more rank than her daughter. What strange things to ponder, distracted by the rain when she should be poring over lists. Instead, Lucy flicks off the kitchen speaker and sits at the kitchen table, the faint sounds of *Jeopardy* from the other room where Doug and Charlie Brown recline. She remains absolutely still. It will be the last quiet moment for several days. She wills the anxiety, tension, and irritability that plagued her all week to subside. She has no idea why Doug invited their old friends to celebrate her fiftieth birthday. It is almost unseemly. Don't most women celebrate their fiftieth with jewelry and a private dinner with their husbands if they are lucky enough to be married at this age? And because Lucy is fortunate enough, because Doug survived cancer ten years ago, she isn't going be ungrateful and ruin her husband's good time. She just hopes that years, distance, and maturity allow these former college roommates to remember the fun of forming a college jam band and forget what pulled them apart.

A Million Miles Away

Gretchen curses when a car honks. Can't he see Gretchen is clearly attempting to parallel park on one of the steepest hills of Mt. Adams? What is wrong with people anyway? She is tempted to honk back but, instead, focuses on her task and, within moments, skillfully parks her truck so the offended driver can be on his miserable way. It's too beautiful a day to be crabby. Gretchen loves the blazing glory of late October. She obtained the chanterelle mushrooms she sought at Findlay Market, and it's not even nine o'clock on a Thursday morning. It's sex, of course. Or at least the afterglow of sex and the promise of romance that makes Gretchen hum the James Taylor tune Logan sang last night. She enters her restaurant, feeling almost weak-kneed remembering the sex they had, right here in her kitchen after her staff left. Because Gretchen's fourteen-year-old son, Walt, was asleep in his bed in their apartment, sex in the restaurant kitchen was the only privacy available. And one needed to be discreet when sleeping with the house musician, the charming man with an acoustic guitar, who quietly performs while patrons enjoy the meals Gretchen herself cooks as head chef while turning the front-of-the-house management over to Nico, who has been working for Gretchen since the start. When Nico, a young French woman, declared themselves a binary American, Gretchen smiled. As far as Gretchen is concerned, they can call themselves whatever they want. As long as they never leave Gretchen.

Her staff is Gretchen's family. Roger and his wife, Venessa are the absolute best cooks in town, able to julienne, sauté, simmer, and stir in a heartbeat. What's more, Venessa has a particular eye for plating, so Gretchen willingly gives her the coveted role at the pass. Duke, the bartender, is so friendly; he is beloved by customers, who light up when greeted by name, something of a parlor trick that results in prodigious tips. John never takes shortcuts on washing dishes, while Nico acts as host while supervising a rotating team of six young, very beautiful servers. Gretchen smiles at the servers around the table at family dinner before evening service but learned years ago not to bother remembering their names. They come and go too quickly.

When Gretchen returned to her hometown of Cincinnati with a degree from culinary school and five years of experience as a sous chef in one of the top restaurants in Manhattan, it took her almost no time to find this building. A perfect brick brownstone split into a side-by-side duplex. Fortunately, the living space for herself, her (now) ex-husband, and their infant son was sufficiently renovated to live in because the work to transform the other space into a restaurant was prodigious. But it was Gretchen's dream to open a restaurant in Mt. Adams. Back in those days, Michael was Gretchen's biggest supporter. Dressed in a suit and tie, he would kiss his wife and son goodbye, navigate the steep hills into the city, and park his car across the street from the Masonic Temple before entering his office at Proctor and Gamble. However, not even the succulent dishes Gretchen prepared to design her menu were enough to keep Michael from Mindy's clutches. Mindy may not cook but earns more money a year than Gretchen has seen in all the years of running her restaurant, which makes no difference to Gretchen. Cooking is her passion, and Gaslight Café, the name she bestowed on her beloved restaurant, is her dream come true. If sacrificing love for work is what it takes, Gretchen does it.

Inspired by La Lanterna di Vittorio on MacDougal Street, a magical café Gretchen stumbled upon in the West Village during her busy days studying at CIA, she supervised the construction of the brownstone to add a terrace garden with a windowed roof she can open and close, the highlight of her restaurant. Metal bistro tables and chairs flanked by potted plants and climbing vines, a stone fountain in one corner, and a fireplace in the other are reminiscent of the New York café. Of course, reservations for that space are always full. What was the brownstone's front living room is now the main dining space. Gretchen designed a beautiful copper-topped bar to fill the cozy space of the former dining room, which boasts a working wood fireplace. The existing kitchen was expanded to become an industrial kitchen. The second floor serves as an intimate banquet space for private parties, and the third floor is for storage.

Next door, Gretchen's home features a living room, dining room, and large kitchen on the first floor. Gretchen plants herbs and vegetables in her small backyard garden that flanks the solarium of the restaurant. The second floor includes three rooms and two bathrooms. Her bedroom features an en suite because Gretchen paid contractors to blow out a smaller bedroom to create it. Her claw-footed bathtub is integral to her nighttime routine. The second room is Gretchen's office, and the third is a guest room. The top floor is Walt's alone. Now that he is becoming a teenager, privacy is increasingly important. Gretchen wishes he didn't stomp down the stairs to use his bathroom on the second floor, but she has no extra money to add a bathroom to the third floor. Not to mention, Walt will only live with her for four more years. And then he will be gone to college. And life.

Fortunately, Gretchen bought the property with an inheritance she received from her grandmother, so it wasn't an issue in the divorce. It belonged to her, not that Michael fought her on anything, really. His guilt for having an affair with Mindy was too great to prolong the agony of divorce. Gretchen was so busy in those days, she barely even noticed Michael was gone. He and Mindy, and their two children fulfilled Michael's destiny of owning a house in Indian Hill and sending their kids to private school. Fortunately, Walt seems to like his stepsiblings and tolerates his stepmother. Because Gretchen has full custody, Walt is subjected to this country club life with his father only a few weekends a month. Gretchen doesn't want to think about how fast time is flying. Walt began high school this fall, and Gretchen doesn't even want to consider next year, he will be driving. Where is that cute, chubby little boy who clung to her side, begging to help in the restaurant? Fill saltshakers, stir something, roll out dough. Anything to be with Gretchen. Those days are long gone, and Gretchen misses him already. What is she going to do when he leaves for college? Perhaps fall in love and create a little romance for herself.

"What are you grinning about this early in the morning?" Roger grumbles. "And where the fuck is the coffee?"

"I forgot to make it," Gretchen says. She turns to the Bunn coffeemaker and pushes the button to grind the French roast beans she and Roger prefer. Within minutes, she hands him a steaming cup of coffee with two sugars, no cream; how he takes it.

"You're singing?" Roger says.

"You're welcome," Gretchen says. As she exits the kitchen, she hears Venessa say, "What is wrong with you? Leave her alone. Maybe she's just happy to be happy."

Gretchen doesn't pause. She already confided in Venessa about her growing feelings for Logan, and everyone in the restaurant seems aware of their flirtations. You'd have to be blind not to, or an oblivious teenager like Walt. Gretchen appreciates Venessa's discretion, although she feels the secret won't remain a secret much longer. Not after last night. Gretchen blushes, remembering how Logan sang an old tune, *I'll Stop the World and Melt with You* to close his set before lingering at the bar, nursing a beer, and shooting the shit with Duke, who was washing the last glasses and restocking the shelves. Gretchen sat next to Logan and accepted the glass of wine Duke pours for her every night before he leaves. No sooner had Duke locked the door behind him were Gretchen and Logan kissing. What she conveniently forgets is the empty feeling she fought after she locked the restaurant door behind Logan. Her bed felt extra cold and empty, lying there alone, wondering all the things a woman wonders after having sex with someone new.

In the light of the new day, Gretchen allows joy and (dare even whisper) hope to replace her insecurities, doubts, and anxieties. Who cares if she slept with Logan? What does it matter if it's nothing more than a fling? Gretchen eats, breathes, lives her restaurant, only carving time and attention for her son. She deserves an affair if she chooses. And it's not like they've always had musicians perform in the restaurant. Logan is the first, actually. He approached Gretchen one balmy April evening at the bar, introduced himself, and asked if he could play for weekend tips. Since Gretchen doesn't have an extra dime to spare and because Logan is incredibly attractive with his long, dark hair, goatee, and glasses, she agrees. Six months was a long flirtation Logan initiated with love songs he quietly crooned as Gretchen strolled the front of the house each evening to greet her customers, taking extra care with her regulars. She smiled when Logan sang *Harvest Moon* by Neil Young, hummed along to *So Far Away* by Carole King, and swooned when he sang *More Than Words* by an artist Gretchen can't name but is a song that has always melted her heart.

At family dinner of chicken and dumplings Roger prepared, Gretchen gazes lovingly at her staff, each so dear to her. It doesn't occur to her that one of the servers is missing until after the table has been cleared and everyone is at their stations, ready to launch the first seating, when Logan and one of the servers walk in together, holding hands. Gretchen stares as the young woman laughs, placing her hand directly on Logan's chest (where Gretchen had laid her head after sex), and then cradles his face as they kiss. And not just a peck. A kiss-between-lovers kind of kiss. Humiliated, Gretchen quickly turns on her sneakered heel and hustles into the kitchen, bypassing Roger and Venessa, and hides in the walk-in before the tears escape.

"Are you okay?" Venessa opens the door and peeks in. When she sees Gretchen's face, she closes the door behind them. "Gretchen, what's going on? You were so happy this morning. What is it?"

"Who is the server sleeping with Logan? What is her name?"

"Which server? Logan, our guitarist? The guy you've been flirting with?"

"Not just flirting. I slept with him—last night. And I just watched him walk in with one of our servers, and they kissed, Venessa. Kissed. Right in front of me. How stupid am I anyway?"

"You slept with him? Which server? Oh, Gretch," Venessa says. She pats Gretchen's shoulder and then exits the walk-in before Gretchen can say, "Wait."

A few moments later, Nico opens the walk-in, causing Gretchen to groan.

"So, who do I have to fire?" Nico says.

"Nobody," Gretchen says, rising and using the corner of her apron to wipe her eyes. "It's nothing, really. What did Venessa say to you?"

"That we have a server who needs to be fired. Did somebody steal or—"

"Nobody needs to be fired," Gretchen says. She pulls the walk-in door open and says, "Let's go. It's nothing. Nobody stole anything." Except my heart, she doesn't say.

Gretchen whispers, "Not a word," to Venessa, giving her a fierce glare. Gretchen fires up her stoves and cooks with sole determination and purpose, not once turning away to see servers carrying plate after plate of her delicious food to the tables. Even when she usually washes her face, combs out her hair, and pulls on a clean apron to walk the restaurant, Gretchen remains firmly in place, cooking.

Following recipes is not like following the rules. Gretchen followed all the rules her whole life, and look where it got her. First, cheated on and divorced. Then, long years as a single mother building a business. And just when she let her guard down, this. Gretchen blames it on that stupid song from the movie *Valley Girl* that evoked a sense of teenage rebellion, allowing her enough courage to believe, for a few short hours, that love was possible when it wasn't.

However, when you follow recipes, you're guaranteed delicious results. Look how happy her cooking makes people.

This is her goddamn restaurant. She resolves to take control of her situation. She's not a heartbroken teenager. It was merely an error of judgment she will have to rectify, she reminds herself as she directs Nico to give notice to both the nameless server and the musician. By the end of service, Gretchen will no longer ever have to look at either of their faces again.

From now on, no more music. Food is enough.

ACKNOWLEDGMENTS

Grateful acknowledgement to the following publications where versions of these stories first appeared:

Cosmic Charlie: *Mobius Magazine* Vol. 34 November 2023
See Here How Everything: *Garfield Lake Review* 2024
Mother's Little Helper: *Action, Spectacle* 2024
About To Run: *Dead Girl Walking*, Red Volume, Wicked Shadow Press 2024
A Christmas Carol: *Pink Panther Magazine* 2024
Back Down to Earth: *Dandelion Revolution Press* Cocoon Issue 2024

ABOUT THE AUTHOR

B. Elizabeth Beck is the author of five collections of poetry, including *Mama Tried* (Broadstone Books), winner of the American Book Fest Prize for Poetry. She is the author of the *Summer Tour Trilogy*. *Swan Songs* is her debut collection of short stories. She was a finalist in the Kentucky State Poetry Society Grand Prix Prize and has been nominated several times for the Pushcart Prize. Elizabeth is a recipient of The Kentucky Foundation for Women grant. Her work appears in journals and anthologies, including *Poetica Magazine*, *Appalachian Review*, *Limestone Blue*, and *Harvard Education Press*. Elizabeth founded two poetry series, Teen Howl, and Poetry at the/ˈtā-bəl/ in Lexington, Kentucky. For more information about Elizabeth: *www.elizbeck.com*.